NEVER LETTING GO

A Town Called
Forgotten

NEVER LETTING GO

A Town Called
Forgotten

#1 INTERNATIONAL BESTSELLING AUTHOR

RACHEL
BRANTON

WHITE
STAR
PRESS

This is a work of fiction, and the views expressed herein are the sole responsibility of the author. Likewise, certain characters, places, and incidents are the product of the author's imagination, and any resemblance to actual persons, living or dead, or actual events or locales, is entirely coincidental.

Never Letting Go (A Town Called Forgotten, Book 5)

Published by White Star Press
P.O. Box 353
American Fork, Utah 84003

Printed in the United States of America
ISBN: 978-1-948982-41-2
Year of first printing: 2023

To my husband, who continues to be my best supporter.

CHAPTER 1

Ronica Wilson stared at the empty bed where her husband normally slept, worry pushing through the comforting numbness in her heart. "Fletcher?" she called. "Where are you?" He'd been here when she checked this morning before she began straining the milk their son Jeremy had brought in from the barn.

She peered under the double bed, hoping he was investigating some treasure his mind had remembered from his youth. This was the same room he'd slept in as a child, used in the interim by the four children they'd raised in the three-bedroom farmhouse. Fletcher hadn't shared her bed for the past year because even if he remembered her when they went to bed, often by morning he wouldn't, and the person who opened his eyes to the world would be confused and sometimes even angry to find a stranger in his bed. This full-size bed in his childhood room meant she could stay with him on evenings he needed her until he slept, though that hadn't happened in a long time. Even on good days, he didn't retain many memories past their courting days, and Fletcher had always been a man of principle.

Ronica hurried to the bathroom to see if he was there, and then to the third bedroom she now thought of as the guest room, where her daughter stayed with her husband when they visited from nearby Panna Creek. Her sons and their families usually stayed with Jeremy in his larger new house across the field, which was okay with Ronica because Jeremy invited her to come over too. He was the one son she could always depend on.

"Fletcher, where are you?" she out called again. Still no answer, and Mars, their old Irish setter, didn't come running either. Or limping, the way he mostly moved these days.

Panic was beginning to work its way into her chest. She searched under the guest bed and in the closet. Nothing. Next was the master bath she shared with Fletcher because he loved the jetted tub in all of his personalities, but he wasn't there either, and the rest of the house was equally unrevealing. She'd put locks on the doors, difficult ones that Fletcher's increasingly clumsy hands couldn't easily work, but when he was lucid, or even semi-lucid, he could still figure them out. He'd always been intelligent. It was entirely possible that he'd left the house, locking the door after him. She checked for his coat and boots. Both were missing.

Should she call Jeremy or search the barn? The farm was under a layer of snow now in mid-January, so it wouldn't be likely that Fletcher would try to lie down in the barren alfalfa fields, and he wouldn't be able to let her beloved Moona Lisa into the wrong field and cause her bloat again.

I'll search, she decided.

She didn't want to bother Jeremy, who already had more than his share of the work on the farm—his farm now, as she had come to think of it. Jeremy had taken the fresh milk and the butter she'd made yesterday to Maggie at the Butter Cake Café, and he'd likely make a stop to see Laina, his girlfriend, who worked at the hardware store. He'd be back soon enough, and someone from the Ladies Auxiliary would be coming soon to sit with Fletcher while Ronica did housework or ran errands. The ladies had been her lifeline, as had her involvement in planning the town events. With Thanksgiving and Christmas behind them, though, she was running out of things to occupy her time.

Time. When she married Fletcher, she hadn't thought the thirteen years between them would be important, but now that space was nothing more than a silent thief, stealing him from her long before his time. If he'd been younger, they would have more good years together.

How could she ever be ready to say goodbye?

Although, that wasn't quite true. They had said goodbye many times in the past five years, and she'd accepted his fate. Their fate.

Fletcher had felt well enough to help her with the butter last evening, and though he didn't remember their life together, he had remembered Ronica. He'd gone down on one knee and asked her to marry him for the fifteenth time in three months, which was far better than asking who she was and when his mother would return. His grin had been wide, his blue eyes sparkled, and it had been easy to reach beyond the thirty-three years of marriage and see the handsome, older farmer who'd courted her so gallantly when she was just nineteen.

When she'd first come to Forgotten to visit her aunt, she had never imagined living on a farm, but she didn't hesitate in saying yes to marrying Fletcher so young. The regrets, however, did come later when she'd had a houseful of babies in five short years. But they'd made it through, laughing more than they struggled, and he'd become her best friend.

Then he'd become ill. Well, there were a lot of years between the two, but sometimes it was best not to dwell on because those were the good times, the years where she loved him madly and deeply and completely.

After his proposal last night, Fletcher had disappeared into his mind before she gathered herself enough to tell him yes yet again.

Ronica bent over as pain arched through her chest like a bolt of lightning, tearing through the comforting numbness, ravaging everything in its path before vanishing. She gasped for breath. It felt like a heart attack or something worse.

Much worse.

But it wasn't a heart attack—or anything else that was physically serious. She'd been to Doc Sayer's clinic at least three times in the past two years to check, and she was grateful both for his reassurance and for keeping her secret.

"Oh, Fletcher," she whispered as the pain subsided, and she could breathe again. "You said it was forever." Or at least until death. But Fletcher had already left her as surely as if he'd climbed into their silver truck and driven away forever.

Or died. A death without a funeral. A living death.

Not his fault, she reminded herself for the millionth time.

Breathing in and out through her mouth in long, steady, calming streams, she took a moment to center herself, one hand splayed on her kitchen table for support. The panic receded, and her practical nature reasserted itself. She hurried to the kitchen door, dragged on her boots, and slipped her coat from the hook by the door.

Fletcher wasn't in the barn. She walked into the barnyard area, scanning the fields. No sign of her husband or the dog, who had become his inseparable shadow over the past year. There were grain silos, however, another barn, and other outbuildings, ones she'd need help searching. There were also many trees that a confused man might sit against to rest and fall asleep, numb in the snow.

She patted her pockets for her phone, only to realize she'd left it in the house. Sobs caught in her throat as she ran back down the snowy path, holding her unzipped coat around her to stave off the cold. Tears blurring her eyes, she nearly ran into Josiah Campbell near her back door.

"Ronica," he said, arms reaching out to steady her. "What's wrong?" His voice was deep, melodious, and authoritative as was apropos for the mayor of Forgotten.

Her eyes lifted to his dark face, topped by black hair that was too short to be kinky or frizzy. As usual, he was the picture of calm, though his brown eyes betrayed their concern.

For her.

And for Fletcher, of course. Kind, careful, supporting Josiah, who had once been their friend and was now her friend and often Fletcher's caretaker. Josiah had saved her sanity when Fletcher was diagnosed with dementia over five years ago, and she owed him more than he probably knew.

Relief pounded through her, and she allowed herself the rare luxury of falling into Josiah's arms. Pushing her face against the soft wool of his long coat, she struggled to hide her tears. She wanted to stay there forever, protected from the stark truth of her life—and from the longing in her heart. But she would never leave Fletcher, and Josiah would never let her.

Josiah tightened his hold. "Is it Fletcher?" he asked in his beautiful voice.

She nodded. "He was in his room before I strained the milk, but he's not anymore. The dog is gone too. I need to call Jeremy. I need to search the farm."

Josiah turned to the house, one arm around her, the other reaching for his phone. "Come inside. We'll find him."

For a stark, horrid moment, Ronica wished they wouldn't. She wished Fletcher would vanish permanently to wherever he'd gone in his mind. He'd left her, essentially breaking the promise of their marriage vows. She hadn't left him in any way. Not when his love for the farm had threatened their marriage, or when the babies had taken all her strength. She'd never been unfaithful, not even when her heart believed she'd made a mistake. Instead, she'd rededicated herself and loved him with her whole heart, mind, and body. But this day in and day out of dementia was killing her spirit. How much more could she take?

Shame followed quickly on the heels of these thoughts. She would do what she had to do because she loved Fletcher and the family they had built together.

None of this is his fault! Her silent cry steadied her turmoil.

"Thank you," she said to Josiah. "I'll call the Ladies Auxiliary. We'll get a search party going."

Josiah smiled at her. "There you go. I'll call Jeremy."

While Josiah talked to Jeremy, she called the hardware store to talk to Pamela Cox, longtime friend and mother to her son's girlfriend. Then she called Maggie Tremblay, who owned the Butter Cake Café and would be able to rally additional volunteers as they showed up to eat.

Josiah finished his call to Jeremy long before she hung up with Maggie, and he also called the police chief, husband to Ronica's good friend, Natalie McColl. "Jeremy's on his way back to check the outbuildings," he told her. "And the chief is getting word to his officers and volunteers. They'll send out a Silver Alert, and I'll text Penny to send out a citywide email. Then I'd like to look around here again, if that's okay."

"Yeah, sure." Ronica had a bright flash of memory of one afternoon when she'd searched for her daughter, her firstborn, who'd disappeared while she had been occupied bathing the twins, both rambunctious little boys, who'd found a puddle of mud to play in. Her daughter had been found sleeping peacefully under the heirloom settee, which Ronica had promptly given away in favor of one that didn't have enough space underneath to fit a curious child.

It would be embarrassing to find Fletcher in the house, but it would also be a relief. She closed her eyes, hoping, praying, and believing him to be there.

Of course, he wasn't. She knew her house inside and out, and though Josiah also searched in the attic and opened storage chests too small to hold even Fletcher's frail body, he wasn't in the house.

"Let's go to Jeremy's and search," Josiah said grimly. "You have a key?"

She nodded, unable to trust her voice.

They went outside and hadn't yet made it across the field to Jeremy's when Laina Cox's pink Beetle sped down the paved drive, barely pausing near Ronica's house as she spied them. She pulled up in front of Jeremy's garage and opened the door so quickly that Ronica heard her pull the emergency brake.

"Oh, Ronica!" Laina exclaimed, sprinting across the field to meet them, her wild, blond curls streaming out behind her petite figure. "Jeremy just texted me. I'm here to help." She threw her arms around Ronica, and that terrible knot in her stomach loosened just a bit. She already loved Laina like a daughter, and she'd kept hinting at Jeremy to propose since they began dating last October, but he'd told her that Laina wanted to get past Christmas first. Ronica couldn't blame her, but they were well into January now.

Her mind caught on that thought. It was January, and Fletcher was out there somewhere in the cold, where snow heaped in dirty piles even after the past few days of unexpected warmth.

"Thanks for coming," Josiah said. "We're going to check Jeremy's."

Laina released her crushing hold on Ronica. She was surprisingly strong for such a slight woman, thanks in part to her training at her family's hardware store. She was a good person to lean on.

"Jeremy had the same idea," she said. "Remember at Christmastime when Fletcher went downstairs and started the fire in the wood stove?"

Ronica did, and it had been a good day. They'd roasted marshmallows indoors, and the smell of the fire hadn't permeated the entire house as Jeremy worried it might. That had to be where Fletcher was now. He'd probably found the bag of marshmallows she bought for the gelatin pudding for Sunday dinner.

They searched the house but didn't find Fletcher or any sign that he'd been there. Ronica could see her worry echoed on Josiah and Laina's faces. They'd stopped reassuring her, and that in itself was concerning.

"Where else should we look?" Determination etched Laina's face. "Where would he go?"

Ronica shrugged. "We have a few outbuildings, but he couldn't have gotten far. My truck is still here." She'd learned to hide the keys. Hope flared again.

"Laina and I will organize volunteers to start walking the fields," Josiah said.

"They should begin arriving any minute," Laina added. "Come on. Let's go back to your house."

"I can help," Ronica insisted.

"Of course." Laina took her hand and held it tightly. "You know the land better than anyone besides Jeremy. We'll make a grid and assign sections."

They were in the kitchen still finalizing the drawings when the first volunteers arrived. Ronica sent them to the north field. She was about to send out the second group when Jeremy arrived at the back door, out of breath, his boots muddy and his blond hair mussed. She could tell by his expression that something was very, very wrong.

"The old tractor is gone," he said, tears glittering in his eyes.

Breath fled from Ronica's chest, and her heartbeat echoed loudly in her ears as she processed what that meant.

Jeremy had refurbished the ancient tractor that had belonged to Fletcher's father more because of nostalgia than anything else. Fletcher had "helped" him in his more lucid moments, though that no longer meant being his adult self. The tractor didn't require a key to start, and Fletcher had been driving it since childhood. There was no doubt Fletcher knew how to operate it, even in his worst moments.

"We'll need to expand the search." Ronica's words were calm, but she clenched her hands, trying to stifle the tightness gripping her heart.

"I'm going to the reservoir." Jeremy was turning as he spoke. "He might be at the cabin."

"I'm going with you." Ronica looked at Laina. "Will you send out the volunteers?"

She nodded. "Of course. I'll take care of it. Go!"

Josiah went with them, calling Chief McColl on the way to give him the update.

They found the tractor at their family property at the Forgotten Reservoir, and Ronica mentally kicked herself that she'd wasted so much time searching the farm while her husband had been here instead. She sat with numb disbelief in the cabin as all of Forgotten, or so it seemed, converged to help search the heavily forested grounds around the water. Laina, having moved the volunteers to the reservoir, sat with her.

Natalie McColl appeared and hugged Ronica tightly. "Have you called your other children?" she asked, sounding a lot like her police chief husband. She was blond and shorter than even Laina, though her chest under her tight ski jacket was decidedly buxom.

Ronica nodded. "Violet and her husband are on their way from Panna Creek. Sam and Silas are away on business, but they're staying in touch."

"That's good." Natalie thumbed over her shoulder. "I'm going to join the search, but I'll keep checking with Caleb and his officers and let you know the minute they hear anything."

Jeremy was already out searching the grounds with Josiah, and he returned to the cabin only when his cheeks were flushed with cold and his fingers so clumsy that he could barely hold a drink. "He's not in the forest," Jeremy told her.

"The water?" she asked, dread in her heart.

"They're getting sonar equipment from Panna Creek now, and

they're breaking the ice. It's not that thick. There's a lot of thinner spots where people have been fishing." His face was pained. "He and I . . . we cut through the ice ourselves last week before it started to melt. He wouldn't know . . ."

"It's not your fault," she said automatically. "Whatever happened." Fletcher was her responsibility. Till death did they part.

"It's no one's fault." Josiah's voice compelled her to look at his dark, beautiful face and understood that he was talking to her guilty heart.

"Right." She took a breath. Logically, she knew it wasn't her fault either. So why did her mind jump there?

The sun was beginning to set over the valley when they found Mars, the Irish setter, floating in a half-frozen hole in the ice, faithful until the end. Two more hours passed before they located Fletcher, brought his body up, and carried him back to the cabin where he was officially pronounced dead. There would be no final words of love, no chance of recognition. Ronica wondered why she didn't cry.

"He looks peaceful," Laina whispered, leaning into Jeremy, whose face was stricken. He turned his face into Laina's hair, his body shaking with grief.

Ronica's daughter agreed. "I'd say happy, even." Violet hesitated, her eyes glistening with unshead tears. "I texted Silas and Sam. They're on their way."

For some reason, this surprised Ronica, though it was a logical thing for someone to do when they had just lost their father. But her twin sons, who lived in Panna Creek like their sister, hadn't shown a lot of concern about Fletcher of late, so maybe she was within her rights to wonder why they'd hurry here now after the fact.

Josiah touched Ronica's shoulder where she sat on the bed by Fletcher's body, which lay next to the Irish setter, both cradled now in homemade quilts, though they'd never be warm again in this life. She could feel the pressure of Josiah's hand but not his heat.

She was numb everywhere. It wasn't that she mourned Fletcher, not really—she'd already done that again and again over these past years. Except for the occasional flashes of pure pain that cut through her like a knife, she'd reached a level of acceptance, but now it was as if her heart had completely shut down.

She raised her head to look at Josiah. "Thank you for being here."

"Of course." Yet for the first time in their friendship, he didn't meet her gaze fully.

What did that mean?

She realized then that he hadn't been scheduled to sit with Fletcher today. Why had he come to the house? Twisting her neck, Ronica studied his face more carefully. She knew he'd recently sent what he believed to be a last amendment to the divorce papers his wife had filed. If she'd signed, they would be done with their lengthy legal battle. Had he come to tell her it was over?

None of that mattered at the moment because Ronica had to take care of Fletcher. She looked at Doc Sayer, who doubled as the coroner in their small town. "We need to take him to the house. I need to do his hair, and I'd like him to wear his best suit at the funeral." Her gaze went to Laina and her mother, Pamela. "You think we can pull a funeral together by Sunday after church? He didn't want to be embalmed, so it has to be quick."

"Absolutely," Pamela said. "With all of tomorrow and Saturday, it'll be plenty of time. Don't worry about a thing. We know what you want—and what Fletcher wanted."

"The Ladies Auxiliary will take care of everything," Laina added.

Relief spread through Ronica. Usually, she was the one to jump in with plans to rescue those who looked to her for help, but in her numbness, she was happy now to let her friends take control.

"Keeping Fletcher here with the heat as low as possible would be better than taking him back to your house," Doc Sayer said.

"Right." Ronica was glad Doc didn't call Fletcher "the body." He'd never be that to her.

"I think we can go as low as we need." Jeremy wiped at his face, still wet and a little red. "The plumbing is well-insulated."

"Yes, but Ronica shouldn't be here alone, especially in the cold." This, of course, came from Josiah.

Violet stood, her face set. "My mother will come back to her house with me. We'll need to get Dad's suit anyway for Sunday morning." She looked at Jeremy. "I'm taking her back now."

He nodded. "I got things here."

Ronica let Violet lead her out of the house, feeling empty somehow at leaving Fletcher behind. But there was hope because she still had the rest of her life in front of her. Decisions yet to make about her future. About Josiah.

There was time, wasn't there? Plenty of time.

Then again, she'd once thought she and Fletcher had all the time in the world.

She glanced back over her shoulder as they left the room. Everyone had returned to staring at Fletcher's lifeless form. Everyone except Josiah, who watched her with concern—and something more that she couldn't decipher but that frightened her. Strange to feel this from a man who had only ever supported her decisions and had been a good, loyal friend to both her and Fletcher for half a lifetime.

What did he know and hadn't told her?

 CHAPTER 2

On Friday evening, Josiah Campbell drove to his large house near the reservoir, a house he loved because it held generations of family memories. His family had been prominent in Forgotten almost since the town began in the late 1800s, the only African American family at the time, and still only one of a handful in the small town. Before his birth, his grandfather had built what they called the Lake House, and when his parents had retired, they moved from their cattle ranch on the outskirts of Forgotten to the Lake House where they lived until their deaths.

Josiah had been an only child, a miracle baby, born to his parents in their early forties. Losing them two months apart when he'd been thirty had been difficult, but his life on the cattle ranch left him little time for grieving—or anything else. And so he might have continued, but then he spent time with Ronica during his service on the town council, and he realized there was more to life than just work.

She, of course, was out of reach, a mother of four children and married to a man he respected. Knowing her heart, he'd been happy when she worked things out with her husband, but it had taken him three or four years more to find love himself in the form of Olivia, his current wife. While she had eventually broken his heart, he couldn't regret their marriage because of Charlie, his greatest joy, and because of his current job as the mayor of Forgotten. If not for Olivia, he'd still be running his cattle ranch, which, as it turned out, wasn't really his thing.

He knocked on the door, as was their agreement, though he still owned the house. Olivia had tried to take it in the divorce, but it was deemed family land, pre-owned and gifted to him. She had taken half their stocks and savings and would receive spousal maintenance for eight years. The stocks and savings had come from the sale of his cattle ranch, which had also been pre-owned, but he hadn't fought that because she'd agreed to live with Charlie in Forgotten until he came of age. She would also receive a generous child support for two and a half more years until Charlie was eighteen. She expected to take Charlie away after high school and make him a doctor, but Josiah knew his son wanted to work as a veterinarian in Forgotten. Allowing Charlie to remain here until he was of age to follow his own dream was worth every bit of money Josiah could pay, even if it meant he currently resided in a city-reclaimed house, now the official Mayoral residence, that was a bit on the scruffy side.

Now everything had changed. He'd signed the final addendum, but Olivia hadn't, and the reason why had shocked him to his very core. He wasn't sure he would survive what the future held, but he'd have to screw his "courage to the sticking place," as Shakespeare had written, and somehow endure what could be more years of hardship ahead.

His thoughts went to Ronica. She was so strong and giving, the exact opposite of his pampered wife, who was one of those women who clawed their way to the top, never caring who they might step on during their climb. There were a lot of adjectives attached to her by most of the town he served—controlling, snooty, arrogant, greedy, mean, cruel, selfish, rude, judgmen-tal—but he tried not to think of them because it influenced the way he talked to her. She was also beautiful, capable, intelligent, and the mother of his child. That had to be his focus now.

"Dad!" Charlie answered the door, his face drawn in confusion. "You're here." Then his expression changed, his smile appearing like a sunrise. "Does that mean I can go with you after all? I mean, it is our weekend. Mom wouldn't let me go search for Mr. Wilson, but I can sit with you at the Wilson cabin, if that's where you'll be tonight. I'm not afraid of seeing him."

"I'm not sleeping there," Josiah said. "That's not why your mother didn't want you to stay with me this weekend."

"Then why?" Charlie blew out a frustrated breath.

Josiah stood in the doorway, studying his son's face and hating what he'd soon have to tell him. Charlie looked a lot like Josiah in the shape of his eyes, his black hair, and his skin that was so dark it was almost as black as his hair. But the shape of Charlie's ears, his thinness, and his haircut—short around the bottom and stylishly upright on top—was all Olivia. Charlie's biggest hope was that he'd grow a little taller and fill out more like his father, and since he was only fifteen, he'd probably get that wish.

"Your mother and I need to talk to you. Together."

Charlie stared. "You're using that voice, Dad. Please don't tell me you're going to let her move me to Lincoln. I thought you had an agreement in place. Can't you go to the judge and make her let me go? You know how I even hate living here during the week now that you're gone. Daaaad!"

Josiah reached out and pulled him close. "You're not going anywhere. It's not that. And everything will be okay. I promise you."

Charlie relaxed, his panic apparently receding, and Josiah was thankful that his son trusted him. Josiah moved him back far enough to look into his eyes. "You okay now?"

Charlie shrugged. "It's just Mom's been acting weird. She's not going to Lincoln like she normally does." He frowned. "Did she break up with that guy?"

Josiah made sure there was no emotion on his face. "I don't know. Why don't you let me talk to her for a bit? We'll text you when to come in."

"Okay." Charlie's shoulders slumped in resignation. "She's in her room."

With another hug, Josiah entered the house, the huge entry tastefully redecorated by Olivia several years ago. She was excellent at interior design, which was what she'd studied in school, and keeping her home and family updated was something she'd always done well. When he had first run for mayor, she'd made sure their family looked the part. It had been overkill in this town of less than four thousand, mostly farmers and ranchers, and almost immediately, she'd set her sights on Panna Creek. But he hadn't wanted to move, and that was when the problems began, because Olivia had grown to hate Forgotten as much as he loved it.

Olivia was in the master bedroom, lying on a couch near the sliding glass door that led to the balcony overlooking the lake. It was one of those lounging couches Josiah liked the look of but that seemed rather useless on the whole.

She'd redone the room—once their bedroom—since he'd left. It had been all white and gray but was now mahogany and beige. Which probably meant styles were changing. He was glad for the remodel, however, because it no longer felt like a space where he'd lived and been betrayed. Once she left, he'd probably need to change things again to suit his own tastes.

Except maybe she wouldn't be leaving. Not in the way they'd planned.

Olivia looked up from a hardback book she was reading, letting it fall to the beige lap blanket covering her lower half. She pulled her bare feet from the end of the couch, tucking them under her flowing, white dressing gown. She looked as beautiful as she had on their wedding day, but now he felt only numbness while looking at her.

"Josiah," she said, holding out her hand for him to take. In the old days, he'd always kissed it, but now he only touched it briefly before settling on the far end of the sofa where her feet had been. "Thank you for coming."

"We have some decisions to make."

Her laugh was bitter. "That's one way to put it. And to be fair, I don't think I would be as nice in your position."

"No, you wouldn't." Olivia would steal custody of Charlie and leave town before the ink on the judge's order had dried.

"Well, let's get right to it, since I know you hate small talk."

"Only when something important needs to be resolved."

She sat up fully then, bringing her feet to the ground. "We can't resolve this, Josiah. You can't fix it. The tumor isn't operable."

"You said radiation and chemo could help."

"To *extend* my life, yes, but unless they can figure out a way to operate, it's simply not curable. Because what I didn't tell you is that I had an intensive week of radiation before Christmas but saw no change. The first round of chemo didn't help, either."

Before Christmas? And he'd thought she and her lover had gone to Hawaii on vacation. Was this another reason she was dragging out the divorce?

"It's been a rough couple of months," Olivia continued, "but I am nothing if not a realist."

"What does Maximilian say about this?" Maximilian was the old high school flame whose attention had given her the courage to face the public ignominy of a failed marriage.

"Max left me. He said this wasn't what he signed up for." Her voice showed no emotion, but the hurt was evident in her eyes.

Josiah didn't point out that she wasn't married or even living with Maximilian, so he hadn't really signed up for anything. Staying with him on the weekends wasn't exactly a commitment.

"So what do you want from me?" His mouth felt dry as it formed the words, ones he hadn't been able to say three days ago when she'd first told him on the phone about her brain cancer and that she wouldn't be signing the final divorce addendum.

"I need *you,* Josiah." Tears gathered in her eyes, one escaping to slip down her cheek. "I didn't sign the addendum because I want to stay married."

The words were like a knife in his chest. How many times he'd wished to hear those words coming from her mouth!

He shook his head. "You can't possibly be serious, not after all we've been through." After all she'd put him through. "Our marriage hasn't been a real marriage for over four years." Since the beginning of her secret infidelities, he'd later learned. "So what is it you really want?"

"I need someone to drive me to appointments, to help me, to . . . I'm going to die, Josiah, and I'm scared." Her voice wobbled, and for an instant, his heart, boarded up tightly against her, felt something.

He shot to his feet. "We're all but divorced. You can pay someone to take care of you."

"It's not the same thing." Her eyes pleaded. "I need someone who cares. I need someone to take care of Charlie close to me, so I can still be in his life. They say I'll only have a couple of months without successful treatment, but with even partially successful treatment and family support, I could have six months to several years. Maybe even four or five."

Years? The knowledge flattened him. "Years?" He paced away and then back again. "Look, I am not unsympathetic, but you have already taken so much, and now you want years more of my life?"

She folded her arms pointedly. "Treatment will be costly, and I'll need your health insurance benefits to get the best care. I haven't had a job since I left the city council, and I won't be able to work now."

"You have plenty of money to pay for health care." Money that had mostly been his before their marriage, but she also had family money from a trust that would pay out in situations like this, a trust for which she managed the investments. And if there was one thing Olivia excelled at besides design, shopping, and entertaining, it was managing her investment portfolio.

"I need my family's support," Olivia said tightly. "And I need Charlie. So I'm not signing the final papers. You can try to force me, but what will the town think when they realize you're abandoning your wife when she has terminal brain cancer?"

"That doesn't . . ." Everyone important knew what kind of person Olivia was, so that wasn't the problem. But he had repeatedly told others that a failed marriage wasn't something to be proud of, though sometimes very necessary, and he believed that. Yet, even if their divorce prevented his re-election, wouldn't it be a small price to pay for the chance to heal his heart?

Then again, he had vowed to love and support Olivia until death. If she no longer wanted to leave their marriage, how could he force her and stay true to his vow? His solemn word?

Because she's only using you, his inner voice said.

Yes, but she's dying.

And therein was the real issue. Olivia didn't have a lot of friends, in Forgotten or elsewhere. The friends she did have were only in her circle because of what she could do for them, since she attracted the same kind of people that she herself was—people with ambition and little compassion, except when it gave them prestige. These weren't people who'd line up to hold Olivia's hand. He thought of how Ronica had texted him about all the food brought to her house; he doubted anyone in town would bring Olivia casseroles.

Of course, even if they did, Olivia wouldn't eat them. She was choosey about everything she put into her body and hired a local woman to prepare meals for her and Charlie, which she left in the refrigerator or freezer each week. Things with low carb counts and plenty of vegetable proteins.

"You find this amusing?" Olivia snapped, her voice sharp.

Josiah focused once more on her beautiful face. He sighed. "Not at all. I was thinking of casseroles."

Olivia blinked at him and smiled tentatively. "I hate casseroles."

"I know." He sat back down, noticing when her arms unfolded, a sure sign that she wasn't going to verbally attack. "I'll help you," he said after a long moment, the words dragging from him like tires over a strip of barbs. "But this does not mean we're going back to how it was. My trust in you has been irrevocably broken."

"But you won't push the divorce?" Her face was hopeful, the smeared makeup around her eyes making her appear more vulnerable. She was still using him the way she always used everyone in her life. Was he a fool to let her? Probably.

The worst part was thinking about Ronica. It was horrible timing for this to happen now. She was perhaps needing him, and his heart ached to realize that helping Olivia meant he wouldn't be there for Ronica in the way he'd hoped. He'd suspected something like this since Olivia had told him of her diagnosis, but still he'd let himself hope. What would staying with Olivia mean for his future? More years wasted with a woman who didn't love him?

No, not wasted because there was Charlie, and he was everything. Though he'd urged Josiah to divorce Olivia and begged to stay with him, he was still a child who was losing his mother. And despite her snooty and controlling way, Olivia loved Charlie. Of that, Josiah was certain.

At the moment, his heart wasn't consoled.

He'd avoided Ronica and Fletcher for years before Fletcher's diagnosis, especially after he realized that his life with Olivia wouldn't be anything like theirs. But after Fletcher had become ill, Josiah recognized that Ronica needed an outlet to give her an identity away from her dying husband and the farm, something she was good at and loved. So he put her in charge of town events and began spending time with Fletcher to give her more freedom. He hadn't been the only one to step up, of course, but he'd been one of the primary volunteers these past five years. Now the memories of playing chess with Fletcher, first in the park or at the Butter Cake Café and then later at their farm, were some of the best memories Josiah had that didn't involve Charlie. He'd been able to put his past feelings for Ronica so far on the back burner that he almost hadn't noticed them. Or at least until this past year when Fletcher deteriorated to the point where he was usually not himself.

In fact, the last time his old friend had made an appearance was one Josiah would never forget. They'd been alone at the park playing chess, and Fletcher's hand had frozen on his bishop as he lifted his gaze from the chess board to stare at Josiah.

"What is it?" Josiah had asked, expecting him to request more ice cream in his increasingly slurred voice.

Instead, Fletcher had spoken normally. "Josiah, you care about Ronica, don't you?"

Tingles of dread prickled Josiah's scalp as he recognized the words Fletcher had already said to him a dozen times in the past two years during his flashes of lucidity. "Of course I do. We're friends."

Fletcher gave a nod. "Look, I have a question for you. Just answer yes or no. There's no one else I can trust, not even my children. They don't treat their mother with the reverence she de-serves after dedicating her life to them. At least my twins don't. Violet isn't as bad, but she's still not all that attentive . . . and kids will be kids. Ronica wants them to have their own lives."

"Jeremy's a good boy. He'll never abandon her. He always treats Ronica well." Josiah had said the words so often it was like reading a script.

"True, but you know what running a farm is like and how much it takes from a man. And he'll have his hands full with a family—at least, I hope he will. I would feel better if you agreed to check in on Ronica every now and then."

Josiah's gut twisted as it always did at this point in the familiar exchange. Did Fletcher suspect that his feelings for Ronica had always been different from those he had for anyone else? Even if Josiah had never acted on those feelings or been inappropriate, he felt guilty for them.

Fletcher grunted impatiently at his delay, going off the usual script. "Is something wrong? I'm not asking you to do anything but keep an eye on her. It's not that wife of yours, is it? She shouldn't object if you unstop a toilet for Ronica or give her a job at City Hall. And for the record, I don't know what possessed you to ever marry Olivia, though I guess I do understand why you don't leave."

What Fletcher didn't remember was that they had also discussed Olivia before, and Fletcher had been instrumental in helping Josiah ease the problems in his marriage—until Olivia stopped hiding her affairs, of course. Then nothing could fix it. Of course, Fletcher had forgotten all those conversations, and it was pointless to reopen the wounds now when he wouldn't remember later.

"It'll be my honor to check in on Ronica," he told Fletcher as he did. "But she's perfectly capable of unstopping a toilet and just about anything else. You know that, right?"

"I do, but she's also vulnerable. She cares too much, does too much for others."

A rush of conscience took Josiah, and this time he said something new. "You might not ask me this if you knew how much I wish I'd met Ronica before you did."

Fletcher stared at him. "Really? I had no idea." He flashed a brief grin. "If that's true, then when I'm gone, you might have some choices to make yourself. Both of you."

"Stop." Josiah held up his hand. He might long for the love Ronica obviously had for her husband, but he wasn't going to discuss it with Fletcher. "Let's never talk about this again."

A laugh burst from the older man. "As if I'd remember."

The comment swept away the tension, and Josiah laughed with him until Fletcher sobered enough to say, "Thank you for giving Ronica the town events. It keeps her busy with something besides me, and she loves it."

"I know. And you're welcome." Though technically, one could argue that he was taking advantage of Ronica's love of helping others, but in this case, Josiah knew he'd been right.

"Thank you for being a friend, Josiah," Fletcher added. "You have always been there for me, and I suspect we will be playing chess long after I forget your name."

That exchange had been the last time he talked with the real Fletcher. Josiah missed him, but it had helped watching over the little boy Fletcher or even the blank Fletcher, who appeared more and more toward in the end.

A sound at the door drew Josiah's mind back to the present. Charlie entered the bedroom, approaching them uncertainly. Josiah glanced at Olivia and saw her phone in her hand, so she must have texted him.

"What's up?" Charlie said, his gaze sliding past Josiah and riveting on his mother.

"Come on in, sweetie." She patted the couch between her and Josiah.

Charlie again looked at his father, and Josiah nodded subtly.

Not missing the exchange, Olivia's lips pursed. "I'm not going to bite. We just need to talk." She patted the couch again, moving the blanket.

"This isn't about the clinic, right?" Charlie came forward, still wary.

"No," Josiah said. "Dr. Morgan says you're doing great. It's a helpful experience and a good opportunity for a high schooler." He half expected Olivia to say something about veterinarians being wannabe doctors, but she didn't.

"Okay, so then what?" Charlie asked.

"Your dad's moving back in," Olivia said.

Charlie's gaze snapped to Josiah's face. "What? Why?" He sounded incredulous, which was exactly how Josiah felt.

"Your mother is ill," Josiah told him gently, placing a hand on his son's arm. "She has a tumor in her head. Brain cancer."

Charlie stiffened, his head whipping back to Olivia. "Are you going to die?"

Olivia's face crumpled as she struggled not to cry. "Oh, honey, I'm going to do my best to fight this. There are treatments, and I'm already doing some. I'm going to do a targeted radiation next Friday. It'll be rough, but we can do it. That's why your daddy's coming home. So we can face this together, as a family."

Josiah's inner voice was screaming at Olivia to tell the whole truth about her diagnosis, yet maybe all their son really needed to know right now was that Olivia was fighting for her life so she'd be around for Charlie. Josiah had to believe she cared about Charlie's mental welfare or staying here would be impossible. There would be time enough later for Charlie to understand the full diagnosis. The boy might not like living with his mother, but he loved her.

Olivia put her arms around Charlie, drawing him close, and he didn't resist as he usually did. Instead, tears began, and he started to sob into his mother's shoulder.

CHAPTER 3

riday afternoon, Natalie McColl dropped the material in her hand and looked at her phone for the hundredth time that day. There was a message from her husband, Caleb, something about being home late, which wasn't surprising after so many of his officers had worked overtime last night looking for Fletcher. As police chief of a small town, he often had to fill in when they were low on available hours.

But the text she kept waiting for still hadn't come. Natalie's loving message to her younger daughter this morning was marked delivered, but Joni—no, Angelica, as she wanted to be called—had not texted back. Again. Natalie wavered between hurt at being ignored, worry that something had happened to her, and anger that her daughter couldn't simply type something like *Hey, I'm okay. I just need space.*

Better yet, she should tell Natalie why she refused to accept any outreach to repair their relationship. After all, normal people fought, and normal people disagreed, but normal people also made up and had compassion for what the other was going through. So did normal not apply to Natalie? Or was it Joni who wasn't normal? *Angelica,* she reminded herself. *I have to remember she's Angelica now.*

Blinking back a tear, she refocused on the dress she was making for a woman in Panna Creek to wear at an awards dinner in Lincoln. The woman was tall and thin, and it was impossible to find a dress that both fit her body and was long enough to be comfortable, so she'd found Natalie by word of mouth.

Once, Joni would have shown her a dozen original designs and helped Natalie sew the chosen dress. Now Natalie adjusted an existing pattern because she simply didn't have the innate design skill her daughter possessed.

That was part of what made their current estrangement so hard. Natalie had started Joni's Dress Shop on Main Street with her daughter five years ago, after the last time she disappeared, but only two years passed before Joni became unreliable. Thinking she needed more free time, Natalie bought pre-made dresses, hired employees, and began doing all the fittings herself, but two more years passed, and Joni never really came back full time. Her behavior was erratic, and she'd started losing weight. She and Caleb had taken her to a digestive disorder center last May, to no avail. When they'd finally brought her home, Natalie found an empty bottle of vodka in her trash, and she'd confronted Joni, knowing it hadn't been there the day before.

"So this is why you can barely get out of bed! And why you've dumped all the dress shop work on me! Have you been lying all along about your digestive issue? Is this the real reason? Tell me the truth!"

"Leave it, Mom," Joni mumbled. "Get out of my room."

"It's my house and my room," Natalie shot back. "And I'll not have you in here drinking your life away."

"Mind your own business. I'm an adult, and it's my life!"

"Not when you live off us!"

And so on. Natalie was embarrassed now at her outburst. She'd wanted to shock her daughter into realizing she had a problem, but it backfired. Joni left the next morning before Natalie had gotten out of bed, taking only two suitcases and her best sewing machine.

Natalie had first begged, pleaded, and groveled in texts, only to be told she was an abusive, hateful mother and to drop dead. After that, there had been no response, not even at Christmas when Natalie lost it and sent a scolding message telling her how much she'd been hurt. As if Joni would care.

Still, Natalie believed it would blow over because Joni had cut them off once before for a few months after high school and then a second time for almost a year when she was twenty. She'd eventually returned when she needed money for therapy and a place to crash, acting as if nothing had happened. But this time it had been almost eight months.

Natalie felt as if her life had stopped the day Joni left, and nothing had been right since, though outwardly she continued to put one foot in front of the other. Every night after Caleb slept, her tears fell into her pillow as she wondered where Joni was and if she was okay.

Every morning, bleary-eyed and aching, she wished she could just stop. Stop feeling, stop aching, stop wanting, stop living. But she couldn't tell anyone that. Not her husband, her older daughter, or any of her friends. No one would understand. They would believe she was weak for giving up. Or, worse, that she was a monster.

And maybe she was. Why else would her beloved child stay away?

CHAPTER 4

onica wandered through Friday and most of Saturday in a haze. She kept starting to make Fletcher cinnamon toast, his favorite, or going to check on him. She would receive updates about the funeral, or Celebration of Life, as her friends were calling it, and start mentally listing what she would bring to make sure Fletcher was occupied during the event.

None of that was necessary anymore. In fact, no one needed anything from her, not even the two grandchildren who were sleeping at her house. They were off at Jeremy's with their cousins, who were staying at his place. Her children were keeping all six of them away so as not to bother her. Part of her understood why because she was entirely distracted, and the grandbabies ranged in age from three to eight and needed constant supervision while on the farm. The other part of her longed to show them the animals and lose herself in being a grandmother.

When the house was too quiet, everything reminded her of Fletcher—the little boy he'd become, not her husband—and it hurt more than she'd expected. Even worse, she began to wonder if Fletcher had done it on purpose, if he'd gone to the reservoir, hoping to end it, hoping to free her. He'd been lucid enough to drive the tractor and had gone straight to their property. While she'd searched for him, he obviously had a goal in mind. Had it been to end his life? Or maybe he'd been the boy, not the man, and he simply wanted to fish the way he had as a child. The result was the same, but believing that he could have ended his life on purpose was driving her crazy.

She had strived over the months to make sure he knew she didn't consider him a burden, especially during his increasingly rare lucid moments. Because the stark truth was that she'd rather have Fletcher in her life in any form than not have him, regardless of the sacrifice that entailed. Regardless of the heartache.

There had been a moment between them one morning shortly after Christmas when Fletcher had come to the kitchen without shuffling his feet. That was her first clue that he was back to himself because he was always careful not to shuffle when he was aware. She glanced over her shoulder in hopeful anticipation. It had been so very long since she'd glimpsed his real self.

"Good morning," she said, smiling.

His answering grin was bright. "Good morning. How are you?"

"I'm good." She searched his face, finding he was the man she loved, the man she'd built a good life with these past thirty-three years. There was a time as recent as a year back when he would have gone to her, kissed her neck, and wrapped his arms around her. But as much as she longed for those times, he'd stopped reaching for her, as if knowing that receiving attention would only give her more pain when he was mentally gone again.

"Liar," he said. "I've been difficult, haven't I?"

"I miss you, is all."

His lips pressed together tightly for an instant, a sign that he was holding back emotion. "I know, and I'm so sorry."

She turned from the milk she was straining. "I have good news." She had to hurry and tell him before he was gone. "Jeremy and Laina Cox have been dating for a couple of months now, and I think they're about to get engaged."

"Little Laina Cox from the hardware store?" Fletcher dragged a hand through his hair in a way that now reminded her of their son Jeremy.

Ronica laughed. "She's still little, but not so young anymore. They make a cute couple. Our son is totally smitten."

"That's good. I like Laina. She always takes the time to show me where things are when I can't remember."

Sorrow filled Ronica's chest at the words, a heavy, swirling weight, but she didn't let it show on her face. This was the game she'd played for over five years. In his lucid moments, she didn't want him to worry about her even more than he did. She had to keep up the appearance of strength for him and for herself, or she'd collapse sobbing into his arms as she had far too many times at the beginning of his diagnosis—only to deal with the grief alone when his illness made him suddenly withdraw.

"Ronica," he said, his gaze intensifying. "Don't mourn me too long. You're young and beautiful. And you're a good wife. You need to find love again. Promise me."

"I'm hardly young," she said lightly. "I'm fifty-two."

He grinned, taking her hand and rubbing his thumb along the back of it. "You don't look a day over forty."

She chuckled, enjoying the compliment and feeling a wave of love for her husband. It wasn't likely true, but Fletcher always knew how to make her feel special. "Guess all those big hats I've been wearing have paid off. And the sunscreen."

"Definitely," Fletcher agreed. "Just remember we've had a good life."

She knew he meant this as a comfort, but the comment stabbed pain into her heart because, yes, they had done something wonderful together, and now it was over, and nothing he could do would change that. He had no idea how many times he'd come back and disappeared, essentially dying each time, because even when he was himself, he usually didn't remember the last time he'd been lucid.

"I know," she said, making her smile as gentle as possible. "You're a good husband."

His hand tightened momentarily on hers. Then the awareness faded from his eyes, and he pulled his hand away, gazing at her in mild alarm and confusion. "Where's my mother?"

"She'll be along soon," she lied because it was the only thing that would soothe him.

"Can I have cinnamon toast?"

"Of course you can."

The memory faded, and Ronica looked around, realizing that she had somehow escaped her daughter's watchful eye and made her way to the barn with her milking buckets in hand. Her pet Holstein, Moona Lisa, was standing in her stall, awaiting her. Jeremy would be there soon to take care of her, as he had been doing since winter set in, but Ronica felt a distinct comfort in habit as she cleaned Moona Lisa's teats and put the smaller metal bucket under her to start milking. She sat on the stool, pressing her head against the cow as the milk squirted satisfyingly into the bucket. Once filled, she emptied the gallon of milk into the larger bucket, also metal, setting it to the side where the cow couldn't tip it over. There would be three gallons by the time she finished.

Sometimes she felt as if Moona Lisa was the only thing tying her to the farm these days. The farm that had always been her husband's other love. Not that Ronica had minded. She had her garden, her four children, Moona Lisa, and for the past five years, thanks to Josiah, she'd been the volunteer in charge of organizing all the town events—with help from the Ladies Auxiliary, of course. She had a firm place in Forgotten, and while her future was in flux, she had come to love the small town as much as her husband did.

Jeremy, of course, her youngest boy, was the biggest reason she continued putting one foot in front of the other each day, the reason she didn't dissolve into a daily puddle of despair at how life had cheated him—both of them. She tried not to let him know how much she depended on him, though. He needed to live his own life, not focus too much on her.

Tears fell onto her lap, and a sob escaped the tightness in her throat. Moona Lisa turned her head toward Ronica at the sound. "He's gone," Ronica told her. "Really and truly this time." The cow's brown eyes studied her, as if urging her to continue. "And I feel like maybe I've done something wrong. Like I didn't take care of him, or maybe my heart abandoned him. Maybe he knew how hard it's been for me and . . ."

Moona Lisa gave a low, plaintiff moo, which made Ronica smile. "I know I'm being silly. I know I did what I could, and I was faithful to him. Except . . ."

Except she did love Josiah, and over the past year as he'd served both her and Fletcher, and as she'd planned town events, she'd grown to love him as more than a friend. There wasn't exactly an understanding between them, but she did crave more. Even while her heart ached for Fletcher and the life that had been stolen from them, she held onto hope that there would be happiness ahead.

She finished the milking. "Thanks for the therapy session," she said, giving Moona Lisa's head a good scratch.

She dumped the last gallon of milk into the larger bucket. The creamy look of the milk was as comforting as sitting on the wooden stool with her head pressed into Moona Lisa's side.

"Mom!" Jeremy's voice was scolding as he entered the barn. "I said I'd do it."

"I needed to. Moona Lisa is a good therapist."

He enveloped her in his strong arms, his frame even bulkier in his winter jacket. "I'm sorry you have to go through this."

"I'm really okay," she said, hugging him back. "It's not like we weren't prepared."

"I know, but still . . ."

She did know.

He drew away and hefted the heavy bucket of milk while she picked up the smaller one and the plastic one filled with the once-warm water to wash the cow before milking. She dumped the water in the rustic sink before following Jeremy from the barn.

"Maggie called and said she's sending Garth over with dinner from the Butter Cake," Jeremy said.

"We already have more food than both my fridges and yours will hold," Ronica said.

Jeremy snorted. "Only yours has food now. Sam and Silas and their kids have pretty much cleared out the stuff you sent to my place. Violet just asked them all to come over and eat here. Some new casseroles arrived that are ready to serve now. Hope that's okay."

"More than okay. I like having everyone around." The more bustle, the more distracted she'd be.

"We all thought you were lying down."

Ronica had to think back. "I was, but my brain wouldn't stop."

"I know exactly what you mean."

The odd note in her son's voice caught her attention. "Did something else happen? Are you fighting with Sam and Silas again?"

"No, they've actually been pretty okay." Jeremy held out an arm to prevent her from walking into a pile of dirty slush. "Well, besides a few comments about how they hated growing up on the farm. It's weird that their experience was so different from mine."

"Well, to be fair, your dad was a lot tougher on them than on you," Ronica said. "He had them working the farm by the time they were nine and was strict with them. By the time you came along a few years later, he was a different man." She and Fletcher had gone through a brief separation during that time, which had contributed to the change. "Everyone makes mistakes."

"I feel glad to have the farm. I really love it, and I loved him."

"I know." Ronica paused as they neared the paved walkway that led to the kitchen door. She could hear the occasional ring of children's voices inside. "If it's not the twins, then what?"

Jeremy frowned, his eyes appearing bluer than usual in the early winter darkness. "It's nothing you should worry about."

"Jeremy!" Ronica gave him her best stare. "Life goes on. Don't shut me out."

He nodded, releasing a sigh. "You know the Whites?"

Ronica knew a stalling tactic when she heard it, but she'd play along. "Of course. They own the butcher shop and have been packaging our meat for years."

"Well, their son Eric is back in town. I don't know if he's on break from the Marines or if he finished his time. I only know he's home because Silas is friends with his older brother."

Ronica was trying to make the connection, and finally it clicked. "He's the guy Laina used to date."

"Not just date. He's the one everyone thought she'd leave town with." Jeremy's face was miserable.

"Well, so what? She didn't. And we both know how much Laina loves Forgotten. And you." Even as she said the words, worry rose in her heart. Laina had become closer than her own daughter in the past few months, mostly because of proximity, and the idea of losing her—of losing anyone else—wasn't something she could wrap her mind around. Time to be a mother and fight for her son.

She fixed a stare on him. "Look, you and Laina have been dating for three months, which I know isn't long in the world outside Forgotten, but here that's a lifetime. What are you waiting for? You're well past Christmas, which was her request, and in a few short months you'll be doing the spring planting, and you won't have time to get married. You need to stop fiddling with that ring in your pocket and actually ask Laina."

Jeremy blinked. "How did you know about the ring?"

She laughed. "You might be all grown up, and I know you're her guy now, but you'll always be my baby. It's time to ask her."

His forehead creased. "But what if I do this marriage thing all wrong? What if she'd be happier with him?" He coughed into his shoulder as if saying the words hurt.

"It's not a choice between him or you," she said. "It's about you and her. Sure, there are many roads that can lead to happiness, but we're the ones who make the choices." She could tell he was still not convinced, so she continued. "You don't know this, but there was a time when your dad and I had some problems. We even separated for a time, and I took you kids to my aunt's. The older ones knew there was something up, but you were only about eight or nine, and it was just a fun adventure in your mind."

He gaped at her. "What happened?"

"I was lonely. Your dad was always out in the fields, and he was tired and cranky when he came in. The older kids were angry with him all the time. They were entering their teen years and didn't want to spend all day working. Plus, I was so young when I married. Barely nineteen, and before I knew it, it felt like I lost myself and became . . . well, my only identity was as a mother and wife, and Fletcher wasn't there for me emotionally. I'd never wanted to live on a farm, much less raise four children practically alone, so I wasn't all that pleasant to live with either."

"Wow. Only nineteen." He shook his head. "I was barely able to feed myself at nineteen, much less take care of a family." He frowned at the milk bucket he carried before asking, "So what happened?"

She snorted a laugh. "I met Josiah."

"Josiah?" His eyes widened.

"Stop whatever you're thinking," she scolded. "It wasn't like that. At the time, Josiah wasn't the mayor. He was a cattle rancher, and a wealthy one at that. He was also a town councilman. He hadn't married Olivia yet. Anyway, some plans fell through for the Spring Planting Dance, and I figured something out, and he noticed my help. For the first time in a long time, I felt appreciated." She gave her son a wistful smile. "Before I came to Forgotten to visit my aunt and met your father, I was going to be an event planner or maybe a wedding planner. But all that disappeared after I came here. I became a farmer's wife, and I wasn't sure I wanted to be that anymore."

What she wouldn't tell her son was that she'd also recognized an emotional connection with Josiah, one she hadn't even shared with Fletcher, and it had shocked her. She'd suddenly regretted marrying so young, before she'd known what she wanted to do with her life.

Jeremy's brows furrowed. "Why didn't you leave?"

"I almost did. Instead, I had it out with your father, and he was man enough to realize that I needed more from him, and that you kids needed more. He stepped up."

"And Josiah?"

"He went his way, and I went mine."

"You and Josiah didn't . . ." He shook his head and looked down at the ground. "Sorry, it's none of my business."

"No," she said. "Your father and I never betrayed each other. We each compromised a little, and for us it worked." She waited a moment before adding with a smile, "I made the right choice. I loved your dad with my whole heart, and he loved me. I was happily involved with you kids, I learned how to garden, and I got Moona Lisa. It's been a fun ride."

"Not for Josiah and Olivia."

She shrugged. "For a while, I thought they would be happy. I hoped they would be." The fact that no one in town liked the awful woman was a good clue as to why it hadn't worked, but she wouldn't say such things to anyone except Josiah.

Jeremy nodded. "It's sad. Josiah is one of the good guys."

"He is."

"I'm glad it worked out with you and Dad."

"It didn't 'work out.' We *made* it work." For her part, she'd resigned herself to eradicating her feelings for Josiah and loving Fletcher even more. She *did* love him, and she could look back knowing that never once, not even in her heart, had she cheated on him. Fletcher had loved her too—and it had been enough until she lost him.

To Jeremy, she added, "It's only when there's no give and take that a relationship becomes impossible. And my point in telling you all this is that you can wait and essentially push Laina toward the Whites' son, or you can act on what your heart is telling you is right for you and for her. She's a big girl and knows her own mind. Yes, she might be happy with this other man, but who's to say she wouldn't be happier with you? Sometimes you just need to act with your heart."

"I love her." Tears gathered in his eyes. "I'd do anything to make her happy."

"Exactly! So let's have a wedding. Before any more time passes."

He chuckled in response to her scolding. "Okay, okay." He jerked his head toward the house. "In the meantime, we'd better get inside. The air feels weird. We're in for a snowstorm soon."

If he said so, it was coming. Jeremy was like his father in knowing about storms. Either he'd been born with the ability, or the land had taught it to him.

Inside her kitchen, Violet had set out the large folding table, and her older three children and their families had already started eating. Laina was also there, sitting elbow-to-elbow with Ronica's two daughters-in-law. Violet's five-year-old daughter, Ella, launched herself from the end of the table in Ronica's direction. "Grammy!" she squealed.

"Mom!" Violet's brows arched high. "I thought you were in bed."

"I went to see Moona Lisa." Ronica transferred her empty buckets to one hand and leaned over to pick up her granddaughter.

Violet smiled. "Good for you."

"I love Moona Lisa too," Ella crowed. "She's be-oooooo-tiful." The other kids laughed at the ongoing joke.

Ronica was having a hard time holding on to the child with the buckets, but Laina jumped up from the table to rescue them. "Have a seat. I can strain the milk."

Ronica relinquished the buckets, following Laina and Jeremy across the room with her eyes. Laina touched Jeremy's arm with a familiarity that soothed her. If he'd just get on with proposing, they'd be fine.

"You want some casserole?" Violet asked. "Or do you want to wait for the food Maggie is sending from the café? I told her we had enough, but she says you'll need more with all of us here for the next few days."

Ronica wasn't hungry, but she knew better than to say that. She shrugged off her coat. "I'll wait for what Maggie is sending. It's probably meatloaf. My favorite." Two of the grand boys groaned their disapproval, and Ronica leaned over to ruffle the youngest boy's towhead. "Good. More for me. But I'd better go wash up since I've been milking the cow."

"Does that mean I have cow on my head now?" Clark asked.

Ronica looked at her hand. "Uh . . ." Clark was Sam's son, and sometimes he was a bit of a stickler for making his germ-loving son wash up. Oops.

"Cool," Clark added. "Now she'll like me the best."

"I hugged Grammy!" Ella protested. "I bet I smell like cow the most." She shoved her arm at Clark, and he gave it a good sniff.

"I don't smell nothing."

"Anything," his mother, Darla, corrected.

"My hands are good," Ronica said, holding them up. "See?"

Everyone laughed, and Ronica left the kids arguing about who Moona Lisa liked the best.

Exhaustion fell over her, which didn't seem right because this was what she loved most—having all the children together in her house. It was what made her consider Josiah's suggestion of extending and remodeling the kitchen.

Fletcher would have loved it too, especially having the older boys back. Before his illness had made the point moot, he'd finally learned to hold his tongue about their infrequent visits. He'd give the children horsey rides on his knee and then real horse rides in the fields. He'd let them feed anything with a stomach, and they all loved it.

The old familiar pain stabbed her heart. Those experiences with Fletcher had been over for a year now, but missing those was probably the thing that hurt the most. That and his touch when he'd come up behind her, nuzzling her neck and holding her against his chest. It seemed forever ago that anyone had held her romantically.

Her thoughts went fleetingly to Josiah. He'd texted several times but had been notably scarce, giving her time with her family. She appreciated his courtesy, but she also desperately missed his steadiness and care.

She considered taking one of the anxiety pills the doctor had given her for emergencies, but then she'd fall asleep and miss out on her family. Better to splash her face with water in the bathroom and take a pain reliever for the headache.

A knocking sound from the front door distracted her, and she passed the hallway bathroom on her way to the door, taking a deep breath before opening it. She was expecting another casserole, but in her heart, she was hoping to see Josiah. Just to hear his voice. Just to know that something odd wasn't going on with him.

She was almost surprised to see Garth Dalton standing on her porch, though Jeremy had said Maggie was sending her husband with food, and she'd been hoping for the meatloaf. Garth carried three heavy-looking bags, and tears pricked her eyes, though she hadn't realized there were any tears left.

"Oh, Garth!" The exclamation escaped her before she could control herself.

"They didn't tell you I was coming?" he asked with a gentle smile. He had very short, dark brown hair, a cleanshaven jaw, and dark blue eyes. Though he wore jeans and a polo, his shoulders were squared and straight, his stance clearly showing his military training.

"Actually, yes. I honestly knew like sixty seconds ago. I just . . ."

He gave her a sympathetic smile. "Understandable." He lifted his hand that held the single bag. "Maggie sent you meatloaf."

Ronica accepted the bag, finding it hard to swallow past the lump in her throat. "Thanks. But you know I have a fridge full of casseroles, right?"

He shrugged. "She knew that, but she wanted to send it anyway. She'd be here herself if it weren't for the funeral arrangements. You can save the casseroles for later. Or save the meatloaf. Whatever works."

"No, I'm going to eat it now." She cradled the bag to her stomach, still warm from Maggie's oven. She still wasn't hungry, but this should tease her palate.

"You can put the other bags here." She indicated the wall table near the door.

He did so but hesitated in leaving. "Look, Ronica, there's something . . . could we talk a minute? I was going to wait until later, but I think . . . you may want to hear what I have to say."

This was puzzling. She and Maggie had been friends for what seemed a lifetime, but he was new to Forgotten, newly retired from the Air Force, a Lieutenant Colonel, and they weren't really friends, not in the way she was with most of the men in her friends' lives. He'd never needed help, and during his and Maggie's four months of marriage, he had been busy trying to renovate a cabin near the reservoir and get his private flight business up and running. She'd also been occupied with Fletcher, so there hadn't been a lot of time to get to know him.

But maybe he needed her now. Maybe Maggie was expecting as she desperately wanted. She was getting on the side of being too old to have children, so that would be a good thing.

"Yeah, of course. Come on in." She led him into the living room, where she sat on the new brown leather sofa she'd purchased last year. It had barely seen use, except for when she and the grandchildren made blanket tents and camped out during their visits. Mostly Violet's children, but occasionally the others as well.

Garth sat on the other side of the sofa. "Do you remember when I first arrived in Forgotten looking for Maggie, and Fletcher went missing?"

"Of course, I remember. You helped him fish and took care of him." Ronica smiled. "Thank you."

He nodded. "It's just . . . he was himself for a little while that day, and he told me something. I wouldn't even bring it up now, but I heard some talk at the café—"

"People are wondering if he did it on purpose." She knew this town, the good and the bad. "It's a normal thing to wonder. He was worried about me." She let out a breath. "I could almost understand if he did."

"No." Garth's voice was firm. "He told me he would never do such a thing. He was worried he might drown accidentally, and you might think . . ." Garth stopped and regrouped. "Look, he didn't want that legacy. He helped me get over my pride that day and forgive Maggie for not telling me about our son before his death, and I promised I would tell you this if it ever became an issue." He shook his head. "I never dreamed it would. How could he have known?"

She gave a little laugh. "Well, I suppose he could have become lucid only to find himself in a precarious situation, so he knew an accident was possible. But more likely, he's told a dozen people different things to tell me, just in case. That was Fletcher. Always planning." He had never really been spontaneous, but she'd loved his dependability.

Garth leaned back, tenting his hands on his lap. "Ah, okay. Well, I hope it helps."

"It actually does. A lot." In fact, her headache had lessened, as if knowing Fletcher hadn't hurt himself to save her pain had eased her guilt.

Guilt?

Yes, and not only from not watching him closely enough. Guilt for the knowledge that she could go on and would. Maybe with Josiah.

"Well, I'd better let you go before the meatloaf gets cold," he said, standing.

"Thank you so much."

She walked him to the door, thinking about Fletcher and his plans. Could that be why Josiah was acting oddly? Had he left a message for her with Josiah?

She didn't think so because Fletcher hadn't been lucid in months, except twice with her and another time with Jeremy and Violet.

But she had to know for sure, so she'd do what adults did when they wanted answers: ask. Now that the decision was made, she needed to decide whether to call or text Josiah. Probably calling would be better.

"Was that Garth?" Laina said, appearing in the hallway. "Because those are definitely bags from the Butter Cake."

"They are. Can you help me with them?"

"Glad to. The kids are hoping for fries."

Ronica smiled. "I'm sure there are fries galore."

Her questions for Josiah could wait just a bit longer.

CHAPTER 5

*A*t one o'clock on Sunday afternoon, the church across from the Butter Cake Café was more packed than it had been at morning services. Maybe it was because of the hour, but Ronica chose to believe the turnout was because her husband had been so well-loved in the community. Maybe even more so since his diagnosis because he'd been a lot more available to everyone coming to the Butter Cake or the park, and because so many people had pitched in with his care.

Ronica turned to Fletcher to tell him her thoughts—only to see her son Jeremy sitting beside her instead. She let out a little sigh, and Jeremy took her hand with his larger one and held it tight, stemming her sudden burst of panic. She'd been ready, she thought, but not for this. Even though Fletcher hadn't been mentally present, and she'd had to make all her decisions alone for months, he'd still been a good listener.

After the pastor welcomed everyone, Jeremy gave the tribute, highlighting his father's life, the good he'd done, and the lessons he'd taught. Ronica had read the tribute that morning at Jeremy's request and had cried a little, so now her mind wandered a bit. She looked at the faces of her four children and six grandchildren. It had been a good life.

Instinctively, her eyes sought out Josiah. She'd already been seated in the family row on the left side before his arrival. He was seated on the right, with Charlie by his side. Charlie looked miserable, as if he'd been crying, and immediately Ronica grew worried on his behalf. She'd heard too many stories about Olivia making the boy's life difficult, and it tore her heart in two. Charlie was a kind, giving, compassionate child who had an intrinsic gift with animals, and with people as well. He reminded her a lot of Jeremy when he was that age—thoughtful, pensive, and hardworking.

What was Olivia putting him through this time? Josiah had stood firmly for his son throughout her demands to take Charlie from Forgotten and when she'd forbidden Charlie to work after school at the vet clinic, but on too much else he'd allowed her to set the rules. Because Olivia was still his wife, the mother of his child, his honor required him to make her life better, even though she had treated him wrongly. This left him open to more heartache.

Olivia, strangely, wasn't present. It wasn't like her to give up the opportunity to make a public appearance and force Charlie to sit with her instead of Josiah. Maybe she couldn't be bothered with Fletcher's funeral. Maybe she'd already moved on. Ronica didn't feel all that guilty at the uncharitable thoughts because she'd watched the torture Josiah endured, especially after he'd understood the depths of Olivia's betrayal.

A part of Ronica had been glad when he'd finally seen what everyone else already knew, but his heart was broken, and it had taken time to heal. Like it had hers. She wished she could sit by him and hold his hand, that she could put an arm around Charlie and tell him it would be okay.

A little hand crept inside hers, and Ronica looked to see Ella reaching over from her mother's lap. She squeezed the little girl's hand. *Thank you,* she mouthed. Grandchildren were her reward for all the years of work raising four children. Not for the first time, she wished she could be closer to them. Panna Creek was only twenty minutes away from Forgotten's Main Street, but from the farm to her children's houses on the far side of Panna Creek, it was closer to forty. But maybe Jeremy and Laina would have children soon.

Her gaze strayed once again to Josiah. His shoulders, normally broad and erect, were slightly curved as if under a great weight. She needed to talk to him to see what she could do to help him.

She refocused on Jeremy's talk in time to hear him say a few words directly to his father. "And that advice you gave me that day, back in October, well, it only means you were still the wisest person I knew. Well, besides Mom." A smattering of laughter arose at that. "So thanks, Dad. I'll take care of the farm just as you would have. I promise. Love you . . . always."

Next, Violet spoke about being grateful she'd been able to spend time visiting with her father the few months before his passing, and Ronica was glad she'd pushed Violet, who, like the twins, hadn't been active in helping out with their father. Then Silas spoke, and the fact that he didn't talk about being forced to work on the farm was all Ronica could ask. Sam's words were even shorter, his words barely understandable through his tears. She hoped he didn't feel too guilty about not coming around often. She knew how difficult it was for them to see their strong father that way, especially when their relationships hadn't been as close as the one Fletcher shared with Jeremy.

Before leaving the pulpit, Sam took a moment to calm himself, and his final words surprised her. "For the record, it was me who started the arguments with my dad that you might have heard about. Now I wish I'd shown him more respect. I always knew he loved me, and he always had my back, no matter how spoiled I acted. And he was always right, though I still hate to admit it."

With sudden insight, Ronica realized it wasn't the past few years

Sam regretted but before that, when he and Fletcher had argued way too often. Sam and Silas had urged Fletcher to sell the unused farmland and the family cabin by the reservoir to pay for down payments on their houses in Panna Creek, but Fletcher had laughed at their demands, telling them to buy their own houses, and it had been a sore point between them for years. There was land for them now in the will, though not the farm or cabin that had long been signed over to Jeremy before Fletcher became too ill, but she was grateful her older boys had maybe come around a little bit in their understanding.

Ronica had already endured a greeting line before the service, so all that was left now was the drive to the cemetery and then the late luncheon at the Butter Cake Café.

Near the entrance to the church, her friend Carina Sayer, Doc's wife, stood with their five-year-old adopted daughter, Amara, who was clutching the blue alicorn she always carried. Carina hugged Ronica and said with a sultry Latina accent, "How you holding up, my friend?"

"Pretty good, I think."

"Okay, that's good, but I'll be calling to check on you. Anyway, Amara's been wanting to tell you something—if that's okay."

"Of course." Ronica squatted down to the child's level. She was pale, blond, and blue-eyed, the complete opposite of her mother. Five years ago, the child had been left on the doorstep of Doc's medical clinic. The Sayers had adopted her, despite her medical problems, but all the rest of Forgotten had also adopted her in their hearts, especially the women from the Ladies Auxiliary. "Hey, sweetie. How are you?"

The little girl frowned. "I'm sad that Fletcher went to heaven because I like playing tic-tac-toe with him during the ladies' meetings."

"Well, I will play with you anytime," Ronica promised.

Amara smiled. "Yay! But I also wanted to tell you that he thought my alicorn was beautiful, and he hugged her. So if you hug her, it's like he's hugging you. That's what made me feel better." She thrust the stuffed animal at her.

Ronica hugged it tightly, blinking to clear the tears that sprang to her eyes. "Wow," she said. "That really does make me feel better. Thank you, Amara."

"Welcome." Tucking the animal under her arm, she turned and skipped through the door.

"Thank you," Ronica told Carina. "She's precious."

"Yes, she is, and I hope it really did help." With another embrace, Carina hurried after her daughter.

Fewer people gathered at the cemetery, perhaps because of the blanket of snow deposited from Jeremy's predicted storm last night. The thick layer of fluffy white muted the world around her, cocooning the gravestones as if suspending them in time.

Thankfully, someone had shoveled a path to the gravesite, and the little snow they'd missed was easily traversed by her black boots. Post-storm, the temperature had dropped, and each breath came out in a whispery cloud.

The pastor offered a prayer, which comforted her heart, but as the coffin sank into the earth, she felt a frantic urge to run and yank the coffin open to make sure Fletcher really was dead and not lying inside the coffin, frightened and begging for release in his little boy voice. Ridiculous. She took a deep breath and calmed herself.

This time it was Jeremy who held her hand. Then, anticlimactically, it was done. The coffin had been lowered but not buried yet, and out of respect it wouldn't be until everyone left. Time to leave Fletcher to his well-earned rest. Her heart banged out an odd rhythm in her chest.

"Mom?" Jeremy asked, leaning over to study her face. "You okay?"

She nodded, forcing a smile. "I'm happy to let God look after him for a while. It's been a challenging few years."

He chuckled. "I think I know what you mean." He exchanged a

glance with Laina, who was at his side. There was no ring on her finger yet, but it hadn't been a full day since her chat with Jeremy about proposing.

"Why don't you two go ahead to the Butter Cake?" Ronica suggested. "I'll get a ride with Violet."

"You sure?" Jeremy asked.

"Yes. I need to stay and talk to a few more people before I leave."

Mostly it was Josiah she wanted to see, before they were surrounded by too many others, and she'd noticed him waiting alone for her, standing near the grave with his hands thrust deep into his coat pockets.

With a hug for Jeremy and Laina, she moved in Josiah's direction, grateful for the black hat and sunglasses that shaded her from the stark light reflecting off the snow. That the glasses also hid her tears wasn't an accident.

Josiah removed his own sunglasses as she approached. "How are you?" His wonderful voice calmed something inside her.

"Better than I thought. It's been nice having the kids and grand-kids around. Little chaotic, though. I've hardly had time to myself. I think when they leave tomorrow, I'll feel it more. The empty house, I mean." She hesitated. "In a way, it's more like losing a child now than a husband, especially after these past four months when he has so rarely been himself."

"Understandable. Either way, it's going to be a huge adjustment. I'm sorry you have to go through this. It's really not fair."

She waved the words away. "I think I left the idea of fairness back in the anger stage. It just is. No one is at fault, and I know Fletcher would want me to be happy." She took off her glasses so he could see what she really felt. "I want to live and love and be happy."

A shadow passed over his face. "I want that for you too."

"And for yourself?"

He didn't answer right away, and she knew her instincts had been correct. He had something to tell her. "Josiah," she pressed gently, "what's happened? Is it Olivia? Charlie?" She glanced around but didn't see the boy there. Had he come to the cemetery or gone directly to the Butter Cake to help with the food? It would be like Charlie to volunteer.

He sucked in a breath, holding it for a time before letting it billow out in one long breath. "Olivia has brain cancer."

Ronica gasped and took an involuntary step backward. Of all the things she'd expected, it hadn't been this. "Oh, Josiah. That's awful. Is it . . . what does the doctor say?"

"It's terminal, and unfortunately the first round of treatments weren't that successful. But with more radiation and chemo, she might be able to beat it for a few years. As for how long, it just really depends." He paused and then added as if in afterthought, "I guess this is really why she stepped down from the city council."

Ronica struggled with her mixed emotions. Olivia had turned Josiah's life into chaos. Some might argue that karma was in play, given how dreadfully Olivia treated others, but Ronica didn't believe the woman deserved to battle cancer.

"I'm really sorry," she said finally. "Does Charlie know?" That would certainly explain the child's demeanor at the funeral.

"He knows, but not the severity. Olivia is glossing over that. You know how she hates imperfection."

Everyone in Forgotten knew that. But there was more in Josiah's brown eyes, a hurt that Ronica longed to soothe.

Josiah's gaze drifted from hers to wander around the quickly emptying graveyard. "Even though Charlie says he doesn't want to live with her and keeps saying he wishes she'd just move alone to Lincoln, he's still a boy, and he loves his mom. I need to make sure she doesn't use this to make him give up his dream."

"Oh, yeah. Definitely." Ronica could see that happening. She followed his gaze, noting that even inside the black gloves Violet had found for her, her hands were starting to go numb with cold. Or was it something else?

Josiah's eyes returned to her face, searching it deeply as he had on only a few other occasions when she'd been close to breaking down and he'd stepped up to be strong for her.

"So," she had to ask. "What does this mean . . .?" For us, she meant. Because though they never talked about it, not in so many words, they both were keenly aware of the attraction between them that made their friendship different from any other. And now they were both free—or almost.

Josiah's jaw clenched, and his wide nostrils flared. "She's refusing to sign the divorce papers that I thought were a done deal last week after I agreed to the increase in her alimony. But apparently, she had her attorney ask for another extension so she could talk to me. Because now she wants to stay married—for the health insurance and family support. I think mostly for the support."

Ronica felt as though someone had slugged her in the stomach. It took a few moments before she could say, "What are you going to do?" She knew he could force Olivia to sign, though she could conceivably open some new concern to further delay the divorce. He'd been generous in his payments to her these past months, and she also had family money.

Josiah frowned. "I don't see any choice. I don't like Olivia, but I can't seem to stop caring about what happens to her." He paused and then said simply, "She gave me Charlie."

For a moment, Ronica lost her voice, as she had when she'd learned Fletcher was ill and would soon be lost to her forever. Of course Olivia would want Josiah with her during her battle. Strong Josiah, who had always put his family before himself, even when he'd suspected that his wife wasn't committed. It was selfish of Olivia . . . and yet Ronica couldn't fault her. Fletcher would not have fared well during his battle without her and Jeremy. Before anything, Josiah had to think about Charlie and how losing his mother would affect him.

"You're right. You have to help her," Ronica said. Tears slipped from both her eyes.

Josiah drew a hand from his coat pocket, moving toward her as if to wipe the tears away but dropping it without touching her. "I don't know what else to do," he admitted. "I know she's using me, but she doesn't have anyone else."

"Her boyfriend?"

He shook his head. "Gone."

"Oh."

Several long heartbeats passed, and then he said, "I don't want to look back and have more regrets about her."

This, Ronica understood only too well. Though Fletcher had asked her several times during his lucid moments to put him in a home in Panna Creek, she'd refused when the doctors said he'd likely lose his battle much sooner. Besides, he would have been miserable there—and confused to be away from the farm and all that he knew.

It would be the same for Olivia, though she retained her mental faculties. She needed the support of family and as far as Ronica knew, she had no close blood relatives except Charlie and her mostly estranged niece, Keisha Jefferson, who worked at the café and was newly engaged to a white man Olivia hated.

"I'm sorry," Josiah said through gritted teeth, not sounding anything like himself.

Ronica put her sunglasses back on so Josiah wouldn't see the new tears that threatened. She needed space from him in that moment, and she could see he needed her to create some. Something in his stance and the wildness of his eyes hinted that he was on the verge of throwing his honor into the wind for her benefit, and if he did, she didn't know if she was strong enough to resist.

"It's life," she replied. "I don't blame you."

Still, her heart felt even more damaged and bruised. Even though she hadn't wanted to let Fletcher go and had battled for his survival, she'd been able to hold onto the underlying hope of Josiah and his love. That hope had sustained her and made the pending loss of

Fletcher a little easier to bear. Now that future had been ripped away.

For a stark moment, she wanted to throw herself into the grave with her husband and stop feeling anything. How could life be so unfair?

"Ronica." Josiah's gaze held hers knowingly, although he couldn't see her eyes, not through the dark lenses. He took her gloved hand and held it firmly between both of his. "I have to do this, but that doesn't mean . . . I promise I'm never letting go." He stopped, and the silence between them was like a scream. "But after everything I'd hoped, I can't pretend that it doesn't seem completely impossible right now. You deserve so much more."

The hurt in his voice was raw and painful, and Ronica understood then that he was going to need her every bit as much as she had needed him these past years. She allowed herself to hold his hand a while longer, wishing they were not outside where she was so cold that she could barely feel him.

"I'll visit Olivia tomorrow," she said. "Whether she wants me to or not. We'll figure out what she needs, and the Ladies Auxiliary will be there. She is a long-time member, so the others already know about her and how difficult she is. You don't have to do this alone."

"I wish I didn't have to do this at all."

"I know." Some people would tell him he didn't have to, that he should walk away and force the divorce. No one would think worse of him, but Josiah was nothing if not good and honorable.

And there was also Charlie. For him, they would both do anything.

CHAPTER 6

The house was finally silent on Monday morning after the busy weekend. Violet and her husband had left early for Panna Creek, needing to get the children to school before going back to work. Ronica hefted a gallon jug of milk, opening her large refrigerator and placing it inside the special crate Jeremy had made to keep the glass jugs from hitting each other and breaking. Many people used quart jars to store milk, but since she delivered most of it to the Butter Cake Café daily, it made sense to send them in as few jars as possible. So far, she'd rejected using metal containers because she loved seeing the white, foamy milk. It was a little silly of her.

Jeremy would arrive soon to take the raw milk and bring back the empties from Saturday since the Butter Cake hadn't been open yesterday except for the family meal after the funeral. That meant she had extra milk from yesterday that needed to be made into butter and cheese. The milk earned her a few hundred dollars a month, which added up, but that wasn't why she did it. Processing the milk was something she'd loved that kept her busy during the times Fletcher worked late on the farm, and it had become even more comforting when he hadn't recognized her near the end.

And later this afternoon, she'd go see Olivia.

Jeremy stumbled into the kitchen without warning, though he normally knocked since moving out to his own house. His blond hair stood on end, and his shirt beneath his open jacket was rumpled and maybe a little stained. "Mom, I told you I'd do the milking. How early did you go? I thought I was on time."

"Moona Lisa is my cow, and there's nothing wrong with me." More gently, she added, "I got this. I don't need to watch your dad anymore, so I have the time. Besides, you were out late last night, or so Silas said when he stopped by this morning on his way out of town." Her eyes sharpened. "Did you and Laina talk?"

He dragged a hand through his hair, which did nothing to fix the mess. "I couldn't ask her on the day of Dad's funeral. That's morbid."

Ronica laughed. "I suppose."

"Besides, I keep coming up with a blank as to how I should ask. I looked on the internet, and they have all these fancy proposal ideas. Do you think Garth would agree to take us somewhere on his plane?"

"What on earth?" Ronica put her hand on her hips. "That is not how I raised you, Jeremy Joshua Wilson!"

Jeremy had the good sense to look abashed. "Okay, then. You're right. But I want it to at least be a little special."

"Well, where did you have your first date?"

"Gandolf's and the theater."

"Well, take her there and propose at one of those, then."

"I do know the owner of the theater. I wonder if . . ." His grin stretched ear-to-ear, and he grabbed her in a bear hug, startling her. "I've got it! Thanks, Mom. You're the best! I'll get the milk to Maggie, then finalize my plans." He turned to the fridge.

"No." She held up her hand. "The milk can wait a bit. Go home and shower first, and make sure you put on clean clothes. You don't want to scare Laina when you finally see her."

"Oh." He looked down at himself and laughed. "Right!" He kissed her cheek and dashed off.

Ronica laughed—and turned to see if Fletcher had understood any of the exchange.

Of course, Fletcher wasn't in his usual spot at the table. A wave of grief overcame her, and she reached out to steady herself on the counter. Strange to feel so lost when she believed she'd mourned him already. Apparently, grief didn't work that way. For long moments, she fought the overwhelming urge to get in her bed and crawl under the covers.

Slowly, the urge faded. She was accustomed to being on her own, and for all intents and purposes, she had lived alone emotionally for a very long time. Instead, she'd take her own shower and focus on what she'd do for Olivia. She'd need to ask someone to go with her to see Olivia because she wasn't going to face that dragon alone.

As hot water sluiced over her body, she felt herself come alive. Her skin tingled, invigorated at the heat. How odd that life went on as if nothing had changed.

Her mind ran over the possibilities of who might agree to go with her to Olivia's. Most of the women she depended on to help her in the Ladies Auxiliary had jobs that kept them busy, or they were too easily cowed by Her Highness Olivia. No-nonsense Pamela Cox, Laina's mother, would be a good choice since she was semi-retired from the hardware store, but Ronica knew she had plans in Panna Creek today to tend her three granddaughters. And Laina was out, not only because she worked but because Ronica definitely wanted Jeremy to go ahead with whatever plan he'd concocted. Carina Sayer wasn't a good choice because Amara didn't like Olivia at all, and Ronica didn't want to make Carina find a sitter.

That left Natalie McColl, who owned Joni's Dress Shop but didn't usually work in the store itself. She sewed custom dresses and completed difficult alterations, but aside from the fittings themselves, she normally worked from the comfort of her own home where she had every imaginable sewing tool and the space to use them.

Usually this meant Natalie had an adjustable schedule, especially when there were no weddings in town, and right now was not wedding season, unless Jeremy and Laina started a new trend.

Ronica found herself smiling as she dried off, enjoying the roughness of the towel on her skin. But her smile faded as she dressed. Josiah wasn't a free man as they'd expected. Olivia was hanging onto something she didn't really want because she needed help. It was as sad as Fletcher and his dementia.

Ronica pushed aside the ache that waited like a smothering blanket and reached for her phone. Natalie answered on the first ring.

"Ronica," she said. "How are you? I've been thinking about you all morning. Are you okay? I was scheduled to sit with Fletcher today, and I should have come over anyway, but I didn't want . . . I didn't know if maybe you wanted to sleep."

"I'm okay," Ronica said, staring into the bathroom mirror, wrapped in a towel with her hair still wet and uncombed. "Just got out of the shower."

"Oh, that's good. That's the first step." Something was off about her voice, and Ronica guessed it was her daughter Joni, or Angelica, as the girl had renamed herself. She was always getting into some kind of trouble. Ronica guessed the young woman was an alcoholic, but as far as Ronica knew, Natalie and her police chief husband hadn't made that connection yet, despite having checked her into a mental facility. They made excuses about mental illness and digestive problems, still believing wholeheartedly in the girl with the amazing design ability, who could take a rag and turn it into a ballgown with nothing but a needle and thread. But it took only one look for anyone else to see that the once-beautiful girl lived a life of addiction. If Natalie had her own suspicions, she never voiced them to Ronica.

So Ronica kept silent, but her heart went out to her friend who suffered more than any mother should.

"I need your help," she said to Natalie. "I have to go see Olivia, and I'd like company."

"Now why do you want to do that?" Natalie didn't even have to ask which Olivia. There was only one who needed no introduction in Forgotten. "I heard she stepped down from the city council in November, which was nothing short of God's own miracle. That means she won't be a thorn in our sides anymore."

Ronica picked up a brush and jabbed it half-heartedly into her hair. "Well, she's still a member of the Ladies Auxiliary, at least for now."

"What do you mean, at least for now?" Natalie's voice tightened. "What do you know?"

"Are you coming with me or not?"

"Of course I am. I got your back. I'll meet you there. But I'd like to know what we're walking into. Does she have the flu or something? Because I can see you taking soup, especially since she's finally going to stop making Josiah's life miserable—at least that was the last word I had from my husband, though, of course, Josiah didn't say it so bluntly."

Ronica's stomach tightened, and the brush clattered to the ground. "They're actually not divorcing. They found out Olivia has brain cancer. Stage four."

Natalie sucked in a breath. "Oh, my lands!" That she didn't say anything more went a long way toward showing what kind of woman she was. Most wouldn't be so charitable. Several seconds passed, and then Natalie did say, "I'm so sorry. I really thought after he divorced that he . . . uh, would finally marry a good woman and be happy."

"Natalie," Ronica began, suspecting where this was going. She hadn't told any of her friends about her growing feelings for Josiah, but they would have to be blind not to see how close they'd become and how well they worked together.

"I know I'm talking out of turn," Natalie continued. "Look, give me thirty minutes, and I'll meet you there."

"Thank you."

Ronica ended up needing every bit of that thirty minutes, though she lived much closer to Josiah's family residence than Natalie, who lived at the edge of town. The reason for that was a little silly. Fifty-two should mean she shouldn't have to worry what anyone thought of her appearance, but this was gorgeous Olivia, who looked down on everyone, the woman who had captured Josiah's heart and made his life a living nightmare.

At the house, she took a deep breath and exited her silver truck to meet Natalie. Maybe it was time to get a new vehicle. A sleek sedan, or maybe even an SUV with room for car seats for her grandchildren. This old truck really didn't fit her lifestyle anymore.

Natalie climbed from her own little car, wearing a gray jacket over a white blouse, skin-tight jeans, and high-heeled boots that were so tall they looked uncomfortable. She arched a penciled brow, her eyes running down Ronica's blue blouse and beige dress pants, both a bit scratchy under her long navy-blue coat. Her brown leather boots were new from Violet, and they pinched her toes since she hadn't yet used her boot stretcher.

"You too, huh?" Natalie said. "Why can't we just come over here in our regular T-shirts and comfortable old boots?" She hugged Ronica.

"Because it's Olivia."

"Yeah, but she's sick."

Ronica sighed. "Maybe it will make a difference."

Natalie rolled her eyes and tucked her straight blond hair behind her ears. "Don't hold your breath. I bet you lunch at the Butter Cake that she comments on your beige pants being a little too white for winter, or that her makeup just isn't behaving today, or some such nonsensical thing."

The words could have come right from Ronica's mouth, and she started to say as much, but a brief glimpse of something else in her friend's hazel eyes worried her. "Are you okay?" she asked.

"Oh, yeah," Natalie said a little too brightly. "And it's me who should be asking that. I still can't believe Fletcher is gone."

"Yeah, me too." Ronica sighed. "But only in the physical sense because he hasn't been there for a long time." She tapped her left temple.

"I know." Natalie's face crumpled, sniffing as she hugged Ronica. Natalie wasn't normally a crier, so that only made her more concerned. Well, that would have to wait because Olivia wouldn't. Ronica had left her a message that they'd be there at ten, and it was already five after.

They knocked on the door, and it was opened by Jill Bier, a rounded older woman with curly gray hair, who had moved to Forgotten from Panna Creek when she married a local widower. Ronica didn't know her well, except that she was Olivia's part-time housekeeper.

"Hello," she said.

"Hi, we have an appointment with Olivia," Ronica said.

Jill looked over her shoulder and back at them. "Well, good luck. She's not feeling well, I think. She asked me to, uh, well, stay a bit longer today to do some things she normally does for herself. And I'm only saying something so you're aware that she might not be up to volunteering. You're from the Ladies Auxiliary, right?"

"We are." Ronica exchanged a look with Natalie before adding, "Thanks for the heads up. We won't be long. We're actually here to help her."

Jill smiled at that. "Olivia doesn't need a lot of help." She looked down at the dusting rag in her hand. "Well, unless it's cleaning. Come on in. She's in the library. Do you know where it is?"

"Yes, we meet here sometimes." Natalie led the way down the hall.

Olivia, dressed in one of her signature pantsuits, this time a vibrant red, was seated in a very large easy chair, upholstered in plush bone-white material, a color Ronica could never have had on a farm with four active kids. But it was lovely here, as were the matching chair and two loveseats that surrounded a large, round, white coffee table. Built-in bookshelves lined the walls, full of tomes that looked as new as books in a bookstore.

Olivia didn't rise as they entered but waved them to the loveseat opposite her. "Have a seat, ladies. Forgive me for not standing to greet you. I have a bit of a headache that's only manageable if I don't move too much."

"They can't give you something for the headache?" Ronica asked, sinking into the soft cushion. It was every bit as comfortable as she remembered.

"My meds will kick in soon." Olivia smiled, but it didn't reach her eyes. Her hand went to the iron-straight black hair that Ronica knew was a wig. Olivia always wore wigs or had fake hair woven into the short strands of her own hair, formed into tiny braids. She normally looked ready for a photo shoot, and today, even with her headache, was no exception. Her striking oval face was perfectly symmetrical, her makeup either tattooed or applied expertly, and her very dark skin was unflawed except for a tiny indentation from a scar near the left corner of her mouth. Somehow, it only added to her beauty.

"I'm so sorry," Ronica said. "About the headache and your diagnosis."

"It's not your fault." Olivia waved her comment away. "You know what? I do believe your pants are almost the same color as my couch. Almost like snow."

"Really?" Natalie cast an I-told-you-so look at Ronica. "They seem a lot darker to me."

"Well, your couches are lovely," Ronica said.

Olivia looked around, a tiny frown hovering on her full lips. "Little bit out of date, but nice, I guess, though I hear beige is making a comeback."

"Good," Natalie said with a laugh. "Because I never updated."

"Well, colors do come around." Olivia's slender fingers moved over a paperback that rested on her lap. "But of course, style is always changing, so one can't really recycle."

"Of course not," Ronica said, finding this amusing given the small and simple town they lived in. "Because companies want more money." She paused and let a few seconds of silence pass before saying, "So how can we help, Olivia? Us in particular but also the entire Ladies Auxiliary. As a long-time member, you know what we are capable of. How can we best serve you and your family? I know how challenging illness can be."

Olivia lifted her eyes from her book to stare at Ronica. "Yes, you do. And I am sorry for your loss. I would have been at the funeral, but . . ." She trailed off.

"It's okay," Ronica hurried to say. They weren't friends, so it hadn't mattered in the least—or wouldn't have if it hadn't signaled a sickness that once again put Josiah firmly in Olivia's abusive reach.

Olivia took a deep breath, letting it out slowly. "Look, it's kind of you to come, but the truth is that I only agreed to meet you because Josiah insisted. I really didn't even want him to tell anyone yet. I don't believe I need help at this time. I have someone to clean, another person for cooking, and Josiah drives Charlie wherever he needs to go. Now that Josiah is moving back in, it will be easier."

Ronica had expected as much, but hearing it from Olivia's mouth made it suddenly real. Not only would Josiah not be getting a divorce, but he'd be moving back in with Olivia. That would be good for Charlie, but taking care of someone as you watched them slowly die was not a fate she wished on anyone, especially not someone she loved.

Olivia was still talking, though Ronica had missed some of the conversation. "So, you see, Josiah and I can handle things very well."

Ronica recognized denial when she heard it. Olivia sounded like she had in the beginning after Fletcher's diagnosis when the idea of accepting help was embarrassing. And how much worse it would have been if she had been the one who needed the help. For Olivia, not being able to control the outcome would be ten times more upsetting to her.

"You just said your radiation treatments are in Lincoln," Natalie said. "That's hours of driving both ways, and then the treatment, which means you may be there a day or five, depending, so you might not be able to come back right after, especially while taking chemo drugs as well. Josiah is the mayor of Forgotten; can he really spend that much time away? And then who takes care of Charlie while you're both gone?"

Olivia gave a slow blink, as if considering this for the first time, which wasn't a bit like her. She was typically thorough with details, and organizing her son's life had always been at the top of her priorities. Was her brain already being affected by the tumor or by the drugs she was taking for the cancer?

"That is true," Olivia admitted. "I'll give it some thought."

"I'll go with you," Ronica offered without thinking too hard about what she was saying. "I can drop you off and do a few errands, or I can stay with you. We could even sleep there overnight. My son Silas has a short-term-rental space there. A four-plex, in fact. And it's the low season."

Olivia drew back with an expression of disgust. "Short-term rental?"

"Yes. You'll like it." Ronica almost added that Silas was as picky as Olivia, but years of experience told her that would only end up making Olivia dig in her heels, and ultimately Josiah and Charlie would pay the price. They were the few people in Olivia's life who were forced to put up with her selfishness. "So when is your next appointment?"

"She said Friday," Natalie said helpfully, which must have been part of the conversation Ronica had missed.

"Great." Before Olivia could protest, Ronica stood and added, "We'd better go so you can rest."

Natalie also stood and took a step toward the door. "Is there anything we can pick up in town for you?" she asked.

"Or in Panna Creek?" Ronica added. "I'm always glad for an excuse to see my grandkids."

Olivia stared at her without blinking, her body frozen, and for a moment, Ronica thought she might fly into a rage, grabbing the mug of steaming liquid on the circular coffee table to throw in her face. But a glittering tear in the corner of her eyes told a different story. Ronica wracked her mind to figure out what she'd said, but Natalie sank onto the sofa closest to Olivia and reached out a hand.

"Grandchildren," she said. "I understand. It's like a punch in the stomach, knowing you might never have any. Neither of my daughters appear ready to ever give me grandchildren. Kenley's already twenty-seven, and she's just interested in work. And Joni—" She heaved a sigh. "I mean Angelica. She says parenting is more trouble than it's worth. When she's talking to me anyway." Much lower, she added, almost to herself, "And in her case . . ." She shook her head. "Never mind." She didn't have to finish because the raw look in her eyes matched Olivia's perfectly.

Ronica sat on the edge of the coffee table next to the mug so Olivia wouldn't have to strain to look up at her. "Your Charlie is a good, good boy. The best. Everyone loves him. He's going to make a wonderful dad someday, and that's something to fight for."

Olivia nodded, a tear cascading down her lovely cheek. "Yes," she whispered. "He's the best boy."

Something inside Ronica shifted at that moment. Before now, she'd believed Olivia to be a completely incurable narcissist without emotion for anyone except herself. But maybe—just maybe—she was a spoiled, entitled woman who had simply had her way all too often.

The three women sat looking at each other. "Aren't we a fine mess?"

Ronica said with a chuckle. "Life just never goes the way we thought it would."

Natalie snorted a laugh, and even Olivia cracked the tiniest smile.

Ronica stood once more, glad the table had withstood her weight. "I'll text you for the details of your next appointment, and I'll let Josiah know it's girls only." He wouldn't like that, she knew, not because he wanted to be with Olivia, but because he would consider it his duty, his penance. She would make him see that he didn't have to do it alone just as he had done with her in regards to Fletcher.

Fletcher. Today the thought of him only brought the numb ache that she was grateful for. Without it, she didn't think she'd have had the courage to waltz in here and face the dragon lady.

No. Don't think of her like that. Thoughts were half the battle. She should know that by now.

Olivia stared at her, either in shock at how she'd taken control or maybe because her brain simply couldn't keep up.

Ronica gentled her expression with what she hoped was a reassuring smile. "Would you like something from the Butter Cake? We're heading there now for lunch and some of Maggie's gooey butter cake. Better yet, you could come with us." Next to her, she could feel Natalie stiffen, and it almost made her laugh. Yes, it was an audacious request.

"Thanks for the invitation," Olivia replied stiffly, "but I couldn't. I'm simply not dressed to go out, and my makeup's a mess. I don't have the energy to do it correctly." She leaned back and touched her forehead with the back of her hand as if checking for a fever, like some fatalistic, old-time movie starlet. All she lacked was the long cigarette holder and white gloves.

Ronica didn't dare glance at Natalie for fear of laughing out loud. There was nothing wrong with Olivia's looks, of course, but Ronica would smack herself before falling into the trap of convincing her.

"Maybe next time," Ronica said lightly. "Can I swing by later with some butter cake then?" She doubted Olivia even ate butter cake, gooey or otherwise.

"Uh . . ." Olivia began with enough hesitation in her voice that Ronica realized maybe she did want the cake after all.

Natalie laughed. "It's not butter cake she wants but your Kansas dirt cake. Aren't I right, Olivia?"

Olivia nodded and didn't quite meet Ronica's gaze. Olivia had entered her own cakes in every town fair dessert contest for the past five years, only to lose out to Ronica's Kansas dirt cake or Maggie's gooey butter cake.

"I'll make you some tonight," Ronica promised.

Olivia looked at her then. "Thank you. I'm sure Charlie and my husband will also enjoy it."

Her husband. Yes. Josiah was still her husband. She hadn't been willing to give enough attention or sacrifice to her marriage to make it work before, but what if she was willing now? What if Olivia lived just long enough to make him fall in love with her again, only to break his heart a second time—or maybe the hundredth time—when she died?

Ronica ached for Josiah just thinking about it, and also, if she were to admit the truth, she also ached for herself. Because things could never be the same between them now.

CHAPTER 7

After awkward goodbyes, they left Olivia sitting on her library sofa and showed themselves out, calling out a farewell to Jill, who was cleaning some figurines in the front sitting room.

"You're making her cake?" Natalie asked, the minute the house door shut behind them. It was colder than the Arctic outside, as if Olivia's chilly welcome had spread to all of Forgotten.

"I know, right? How did that happen?"

"Girl, you just lost your husband. Oh, I know you've already made your peace with his illness after so many years, but you shouldn't have to be making a cake or driving Miss Olivia Higher-than-thou anywhere."

"Natalie!" Ronica looked back at the house, half expecting to see Olivia hanging out a window eavesdropping, but she was probably still in the library resting.

"It's true, and did you notice she mentioned both your pants and her makeup? I about snorted right then."

"No, you didn't. You were kind." Ronica stopped walking. "How did you know about the grandchild thing?"

Natalie sobered. "If she really is dying, it'll be something she'll miss for sure. What she doesn't realize is that Charlie won't ever leave this town except to become a vet, and then he'll be back, so even if she didn't have cancer, she likely wouldn't be too involved in her grandchildren's lives because she'd insist the relationship be on her terms. Their situation has estrangement written all over it."

"You're probably right."

Natalie nodded before saying quietly, "And that's a living death I don't wish on anyone, not even Olivia."

Ronica pondered that as she drove to the Butter Cake Café on Main Street, where the owner herself waited on them. Maggie Trembley was slender and beautiful in an earthy, abandoned way, with a thick mound of raven hair pulled up on her head and kind eyes almost as equally dark.

"Welcome, ladies," Maggie greeted them. "Good timing. You've just beaten the lunch rush. It's on the house, by the way, so have whatever you want." Her voice was like silk. In another lifetime she'd been a famous singer, and after many years away from that part of her life, she was finally working on a new album that she planned to release as an indie artist.

"No, I couldn't." Ronica held up a hand. "You've already done so much with planning the funeral and the food yesterday. And what Garth brought over."

Maggie put her hands on her hips. "Don't tell me what I can or can't do for you. Ronica, you are one of my best friends, and Fletcher was too. I'm so sorry." Tears gathered in her eyes as she came around the counter and hugged Ronica.

"Thanks." Ronica fought her own tears, though she didn't know why. She didn't hurt inside right now. Maybe it was because of the love and support everyone offered.

Natalie had gone silent, but when they were ensconced with their food in the deserted L-section near the back door, she said, "I'm glad you have everyone to help you through this. Everyone understands the pain and can imagine what you're going through. It's a help, isn't it? I'm glad for you." The words were almost fierce.

Ronica tilted her head to better study her friend. Something was odd, something that she couldn't yet pin down. "Yes," she agreed. "It does help, and it's been helping for a long time, especially these past six months. But what's going on with you? Why are you . . . ? You're acting different."

"I've lost her again."

Ronica laid her fork by her salad. "Joni?" she guessed. "I mean Angelica."

Natalie nodded. "Two times before she disappeared from my life, and I didn't know if she was alive or dead. I literally had to think of her as dead and throw myself into some project that took all my time. Then we'd get a call from her, asking to come home or to pay for some therapy or whatever. We never really knew what we were paying for, but we always went to help her when she asked. I would put a box around my heart, so I wouldn't—" She broke off as her voice cracked. "She'd act as if nothing ever happened and that I was the most wonderful mother in the world."

"Until the next time," Ronica said sympathetically, already knowing the story.

Natalie nodded. "You know last May she was having digestive problems, and we paid for her to get therapy." She sighed before starting again. "What I didn't tell you was that when I saw her, she was way too thin. It was scary and upsetting. Someone mentioned something about addiction, but I asked her, and she said no." Her hands clenched and unclenched on top of the table.

"You think she'd tell you the truth?" Ronica was doubtful.

Natalie nodded, then shook her head. "I did, but I don't anymore. Stupid, isn't it? She's lied since she could walk, and her daddy becoming the police chief when she was in high school didn't slow her down one bit." Her face flushed as she swallowed noisily. "I'm her mother, and I love her so much. I didn't think she would lie to me, but I knew something wasn't right. Then I found an empty bottle of vodka in her trash when it had been emptied the day before, and I confronted her. She blew up, telling me to mind my own business, and I haven't heard from her since besides a few really mean texts telling me what a horrid, abusive parent I am and that she's just realized how I've never been there for her. Caleb refused to give her money when she texted him, so she cut him off too."

She looked around the café as if making sure they couldn't be overheard, but their immediate vicinity was still vacant. "It's already been nearly eight months for this third estrangement, and I think I'm never going to see her again. I'm so hurt and terribly ashamed. What kind of mother gets cut off by her own child? It feels like she died. Like she's gone forever, but there's no one I can talk to about it because she's gone by choice, and no one understands. Mothers like me must be abusive and crazy, because how can we be anything else? It's all our fault—it's always our fault. And we're supposed to be strong and keep reaching out and having our hearts stomped on repeatedly because we're the parents."

"Why didn't you say something?" Ronica asked, reaching across the table to take her hand. "I'm so sorry for not being there for you."

Natalie shook her head. "You had enough on your plate. Besides, I'm so embarrassed. It's not like the last two times when she just disappeared without a word. I said things I probably shouldn't have, and she was so hateful in return." She paused, looking around again. "I tried to tell my sisters because they know everything and how she's been over the years, but they keep saying to forget her, to walk away and be glad, and to let her be. But how can one write off a child? It feels like I'm dying inside, bit by bit. And what if someday she has a child, and I never get to see my grandbaby? She could already have one by now, despite what she says about not wanting to bring a child into this rotten world." Natalie sucked in a convulsive sob and looked around again before saying in a harsh whisper, "There are days when I just want to die. Most days, in fact. If it weren't for Caleb and Kenley, I don't know what I might do."

Ronica didn't know what to say, but she did understand at least a little. Her older sons had been distant for years now, and though they hadn't cut her off, she walked very carefully around them because she'd seen how they treated Fletcher before his illness. Yes, it was partly his fault, but not all of it, not by a long shot. But the shame . . . yes, she understood that part.

"Aw, sweetie," she murmured. "That's got to be the hardest thing in the world."

Natalie convulsed with another sob. "Except if she actually died, I guess. But it doesn't feel that way. Hope . . . it hurts so much. Like all my insides are exposed, and anything anyone says hurts more." Her lips pressed together tightly, and her face crumpled. "God, please just take me. I can't do this anymore."

"No, no." Ronica left her chair across from Natalie to slide into the one next to her, placing her arm around her friend. "Like you said, there's no support for this situation. No understanding. No help. No wonder you feel so desperate. But I'm here for you, and I am so sorry."

Natalie leaned into her, silent tears dripping down her face. For long moments, they simply sat together until Natalie calmed. "I'm sorry," she muttered. "I didn't mean to fall apart in front of you like this. I'm just worried about her, and I'm so hurt. I know I'll never be able to trust her again, but at the same time it feels like no one in this world will ever stay in her life long enough to love her as much as I do. I hope that's wrong." The last words came on a shuddering breath.

"You don't know where she is?"

She shook her head. "She hasn't called or texted, not even for my birthday." She gave a sharp, twisted laugh. "Of course, she doesn't even know when my birthday is. Or my favorite color, my favorite food, or what I like to do." Her voice lowered even further. "I guess she doesn't know anything about me really."

Ronica rubbed her back. "Well, does Kenley know all that? Because my older boys certainly don't. Well, if they do know my birthday, it's only because they put it in their phones."

"Joni doesn't care enough to do that. I don't matter as a person. Do you know how many Mother's Days I haven't received a text or phone call? Or even a card? But none of that matters to me, not really. I just want her back. I want her to know I love her."

"She has to know. After all you've done."

Natalie shook her head. "She doesn't see any of it. I think that's the biggest hurt of all—when you understand that the child you've loved and sacrificed for has zero emotion toward you and acts so cruelly." Despite the words, Natalie was calm now, as if drained and too depressed to find enough energy to cry.

"We'll figure something out," Ronica promised.

"Maybe I deserve it all." Natalie's voice was monotone now. "Maybe I really am a terrible, awful person."

"No way. And I've known you a lot longer than your daughter has. I know your heart. You don't deserve this. No one does. The fact is that Joni is troubled. Maybe she has to come to that understanding herself, so she can get the help she needs."

"I don't know." Natalie lifted her eyes to meet Ronica's. "But it does make me feel better to talk about it. I can't really talk to Caleb because his heart is so hard against her now for what she's done to both of us. Our family is literally destroyed."

"Well, I'm here anytime, but you should talk to him. Don't let it get between you. I've seen the way he treats you. That man loves you something fierce."

"He's sweet, and he tries. But now that we believe she's an

alcoholic, and maybe even using drugs, he sees her as one of his criminals."

"That's a consequence," Ronica said firmly. "But you know as well as I do that the next time she calls, he'll be there to help her."

"I wish I didn't want her to call. I wish I could stop loving her, that I could turn off my feelings like she can."

Ronica didn't know what to say about that. The ability to turn off feelings would have come in handy for her these past few years as well. "And Kenley? How is she taking all this?"

"She told Joni to grow up and stop acting like a jerk, and Joni blocked her on everything too. So now Joni doesn't even have her to talk to. I shouldn't have let Kenley know."

Ronica's anger grew at the hurt in her friend's voice. "More consequences. Joni doesn't get to control who you talk to if she doesn't even want to be in the conversation, and you're not the abuser here. She is, even if she doesn't see it. The silent treatment is abuse. You know that. Look, death or no death, you're going through the grieving process. You'll get where you need to be, but in the meantime, you do need support. Would you be okay with me looking into some ideas I have? Discreetly, of course."

Natalie shrugged. "I guess. But I saw a therapist. He basically said that if I want a relationship with her, I have to take all the blame because I'm the parent. I am willing to do that, or at least apologize profusely for any hurts I've caused her—because I am desperately sorry—but how can I if she refuses to talk?"

"What has this world come to?" Ronica gave her another one-arm hug as she glanced at some construction workers heading their way. "Why don't you tell me about Kenley? Is she still working as an epidemiologist? What project is she on now?" She slipped back to the other side of the table, which had the added benefit of blocking Natalie's face from the view of the workers who were settling at a table behind Ronica's back.

Her questions about Kenley were enough to pull Natalie back

from the darkness as she talked lovingly about her older daughter, who had moved away because of her career, but who called often and came to visit for holidays. If she ever did have children, she would surely want them to know their grandparents, and that was part of what kept Natalie from giving in to utter despair.

They finished lunch with considerably less drama, and Ronica made it out of the nearly deserted Butter Cake without anyone stopping to give their condolences.

"Please let me know if you want some company on those trips with Olivia," Natalie said as they walked to their vehicles. "I have sewing I can always take with me, and that would make it two against one."

Ronica shot her a grin. "So we'd only need two or three more ladies to make it even."

Natalie slapped her leg and let out a huge guffaw. "You are so good for me. Thank you for calling today."

"We're all in this thing together. Life, I mean."

They said goodbye, and Ronica drove down Main Street, but only to Terrell's, located on the other side of the city park next to the Butter Cake. She needed the French vanilla pudding Terrell always stocked just for her so that her Kansas dirt cake turned out perfectly. Her recipe had most of the usual ingredients like cream cheese, milk, butter, sandwich cookies, and sugar, but she'd tweaked it enough that it wasn't really typical anymore. She used powdered sugar and only a little bit of cream cheese because Jeremy hadn't liked it as a child, and she always used both butter and margarine. She also added the thinnest layer of brownie-like, homemade chocolate cake as the middle layer between the final pudding mixture and the crushed cookies. She'd done that the first time so she could enter it in a baking contest since most dirt cakes never saw the inside of an oven. She'd won that year and many others. Sometimes for the kids' birthdays, she added gummy worms, but that wouldn't do for Olivia. Maybe she had a few fancy candy flowers left in the freezer from the last Ladies Auxiliary luncheon.

At first Ronica felt odd being in town without Fletcher as her shadow, but at the same time it was also liberating. She didn't have to keep looking around to make sure he wasn't stacking cans, making little piles of salt, toilet papering the bathroom, or rudely demanding cinnamon toast from strangers. It was the same feeling as when she'd left Sam and Silas, then active two-year-olds, for the first time at home with a trusted sitter. She'd felt like a different person without her attention divided in a million different directions. Except now there was no sitter, and she wouldn't be going home to give Fletcher a hug and a treat.

I'm sorry, Fletcher. Sorry that she felt free and relieved without him. Yes, given the chance, she'd want him back because she loved him, but her life had been put on hold these past years. And now she had to figure out what to do next—especially with Josiah and Olivia getting back together. Josiah had become her best friend, and she depended on him, but somehow that didn't seem appropriate now.

She needed a new focus. The town's Valentine Dance, held at the high school every year, was next on the calendar, but she had already finished the planning. So that meant she had time to look into support for Natalie. And yes, she could drive Olivia to her appointments. As much as she dreaded it, she owed Josiah more than she could ever repay for his kindnesses to her and Fletcher over the many years.

As she drove down Main Street on her way out of town, she caught a glimpse of Jeremy's bright blue Ford truck in the parking lot of the theater. Hope shot through her. Maybe he was serious about proposing, and maybe it was happening today. A marriage would be the perfect focus for her, and for Jeremy too. She loved Laina, and having her as a daughter-in-law would be amazing, not only because Laina's dream was to raise half a dozen fat babies but because she was a down-to-earth, solid person who didn't play silly games or nurse hurt feelings. Ronica would be more than happy to jump right in with Laina and her mother to give Laina the wedding she'd always wanted—whatever that was.

Ronica couldn't help smiling all the way home.

Her smile faded when she spied Josiah's dark blue sedan parked outside her house. He was still in the car as she opened the garage and drove inside. It wasn't unusual for him to stop by during his lunch hour to check on her and Fletcher, but now that Fletcher was gone, and he was staying with Olivia, she hadn't expected to see him here again.

Had he already knocked, or was he debating whether or not to walk up to the door? Either way, he hadn't called or texted to warn her, and that wasn't like him.

Plastering a smile on her face, she climbed from the car and went to meet him.

CHAPTER 8

Laina Cox was puzzled at Jeremy's cryptic message about needing to show her something at the theater, but she was glad to take a break. Her mother just happened to appear at the Hammer and Nails after lunch even though her father and brother, Wyatt, were working too, so she wasn't really needed there at the moment.

Anticipation rose inside her. Maybe Jeremy had arranged a pre-viewing of a movie that was coming to town. With all that had happened over the weekend, she wasn't up on new releases that might be finally making their way to Forgotten. Last week, they'd driven all the way to Lincoln to see a show they'd both been too impatient to wait for. Of course they would see it again once it hit Forgotten because they wanted to support the local theater. As business owners, her family understood what it meant to have community support and how that same support also helped the individuals living here. Losing businesses hurt everyone in the long run and limited their choices.

The love of community was one of the reasons she never wanted to leave Forgotten, though she had to admit she felt a shot of travel envy when Eric White appeared at the hardware store that morning. He was as handsome as ever, though more filled out than he'd been before joining the Marines, and his magnetism grew as he talked enthusiastically of places he'd seen during his service. Had she not broken up with him, she could have been a part of that.

She could also have been a widow. Losing her brother to the military had been enough for a lifetime. Besides, she was completely in love with Jeremy. He was her future, though lately he'd been acting strange, distant even. Maybe it was time to confront him because she wasn't going to wait around much longer. She hadn't wanted a Christmas proposal, but Christmas was long over. Now they'd waited so long that his father couldn't be a part of it. Did that bother him? Did he blame her for not getting engaged earlier?

Pushing the thoughts aside, she crossed Main Street and circled around the theater to the back door that led directly into the stadium seating as per his instructions. The theater was dark enough that she had to blink several times to get her bearings.

"Jeremy?" she called out. The theater seemed to be empty.

"Here." A phone light went on a few rows down from the center of the seats—her favorite sitting place, as opposed to his three or four rows back.

She grinned and reached for her own phone to use the flashlight function, though her eyes were quickly adjusting and the dim lights along the seats became visible. When she reached him, he stood to kiss her, holding her tightly.

"What's this?" she asked. "A private movie showing? You find a killer shark movie I don't know about?"

He laughed, and she detected a hint of nervousness. "Something like that." He kissed her again.

"No popcorn?" she teased.

"I have *something better.*" He motioned to a closed popcorn carton on the seat next to his, the kind she knew came with the small children's snack boxes. This was strange as they normally bought the large buckets.

Something tilted inside her. Something better. Could that mean what she thought it might? Her heart rate accelerated. She couldn't be more grateful for the darkness that hid her sudden flush.

"Cool," she said calmly, when she really wanted to squeal like a little girl.

He kissed her once more, and she could feel his tension now. Strangely, that made her relax because more than anything else in the world, she trusted him.

Unnecessarily, he helped her sit, then he waved at the back of the theater, and something appeared on the big screen: a huge number ten. It changed to a nine as the numbers counted slowly downward like the precursor to some vintage film. Had he found some old movie to show her? That would be cool, though a decided letdown after where her thoughts had gone.

Then Jeremy's face appeared on the screen, almost shocking her with how large it was. "Hey, Laina," the movie Jeremy said. "Thanks for coming." He paused.

She glanced over at the real Jeremy. "Um, you're welcome?"

He took her hand and squeezed, looking back at the big screen as movie Jeremy said, "I brought you here because there's something I've been wanting to say to you for a very long time."

The camera lens zoomed out until all of movie Jeremy was on the screen. He knelt and pulled out a small velvet box, opening it to show a ring. "Laina Andrea Cox, I love you with my whole heart. Will you do me the honor of becoming my wife? I promise to do everything in my power to make you happy." The movie Jeremy froze in place, waiting, waiting, waiting.

Drawing in a quick breath, she looked at the real Jeremy, who had somehow wedged himself between the rows of seats next to where she sat, kneeling like the movie Jeremy. In his hand, he held not a ring box but the popcorn box. She took it a bit unsteadily, opening it to find a ring lying atop buttery movie popcorn. As she tried to get it out, it sank deeper, and she had to let most of the popcorn fall to the floor and her lap as she shook it out onto her hand. It was the ring she'd admired months ago when they'd gone looking and she told him it had better not be her Christmas gift.

Laughing, she leaned over to kiss him. "Of course I will! I love you too." She handed him the ring, and he slid it onto her finger before taking both of her hands in his.

"I meant what I said about making you happy," he said. "I know it takes two willing people to make a relationship work, and that's what I'm promising. I will always be willing. And if you think I'm not, you can sic my mom on me, and she'll straighten me out quick."

Laina laughed. "Half of why I said yes is because of your mom and how you treat her. You're a good man, Jeremy Joshua Wilson, and I will be honored to have you as my husband."

They kissed again, much more deeply than before, with him still kneeling and her sitting, the buttery popcorn in her lap and under his knees. It didn't matter. Nothing mattered but his mouth on hers. The world had ceased to exist.

After a while, she became aware of the movie Jeremy still staring at them, caught in a soulful expression. The hovering presence reminded her that someone had been involved in projecting the movie recording onto the screen, so they weren't really alone.

She flicked her gaze to the screen. "We should give movie Jeremy a break and go tell my mom."

"Movie Jeremy?"

"Yeah." She grinned. "Come on." She gave his arm a tug.

"No," he said. "Not before we have a date to tell our mothers. That is one thing I don't want to have them bugging us about."

"Okay, how about next month on Valentine's Day?" she said without hesitation.

He arched a brow. "Wouldn't you prefer another day that was just ours? I mean, you did kind of make a big deal about not getting engaged on Christmas."

"That's different," she said with a laugh. "An anniversary is both of us celebrating our love. Getting an engagement ring on Christmas Day seems too much like the engagement being a gift just for me, not both of us, which I know is silly, but I still feel that way. Even celebrating a wedding anniversary at Christmas would be preferable to getting engaged then."

"Okay, I get it." He leaned over and kissed her forehead. "To tell the truth, it's kind of smart. I want to always remember our anniversary, and this way it'll be impossible to forget."

She laughed. "Glad I can make it easy for both of us."

"Another reason I love you so much." He kissed her again before rising to his feet, bringing her with him, and leading her out of the theater.

Laina was floating on so much happiness, her feet barely seemed to touch the ground as they emerged into the parking lot. But then she remembered. "Oh, I forgot to tell you. Several people mentioned it today at the store, so I think it's a valid rumor. I was going to text you about it, but it's not really something I wanted to say in a text." She paused for a breath. "They say Josiah is moving back in with Olivia and Charlie."

He stopped walking, his eyes growing large. "What? But I thought Josiah sent her the final addendum. He gave her everything she asked for except the house."

"I know. I was there when he told us last week." She shrugged. "It doesn't make any sense."

"I thought my mom and Josiah . . ." He didn't have to finish.

"Me too." Laina had seen the love between the couple, love that she'd hoped would come to something. Maybe not soon but eventually. They'd both already suffered and lost so much.

Jeremy took her hand and kissed it. "My mom's a rock, but losing my dad . . . I don't know how she could have faced that without Josiah. I need to talk to her."

"Of course you do." She gave him an encouraging smile. "And I have to get back to work." She held up her hand with the engagement ring. "Should I hide this until later so we can tell my parents together?"

He shook his head. "I asked them weeks ago for their blessing, and I called them about today. Why do you think your mom came to the store?"

"Oh, okay." She gave him a grin. "Then they'll be waiting for us."

"Right. I'll go with you first, and then we can go to my mom's."

Laina made a face. "I'm not sure talking to her about Josiah with me there is a good idea."

"But we have to tell her about the engagement."

"Before the town grapevine does, you mean. Right. I can wait at your house until you tell me to come over."

"Our house," he corrected. "You're going to move in with me, right?"

She batted her eyes at him. "Only after the wedding."

"That's what I meant. I know your father has at least a dozen guns." They both laughed.

Leaving his truck where it was, they went on foot to the Hammer and Nails. So far, this was the happiest day of Laina's life. Yet she couldn't help worrying about her future mother-in-law.

What was going on with Josiah?

CHAPTER 9

Josiah sat at Ronica's kitchen table where he had played chess so many times with Fletcher. His shoulders felt heavy and his movements slow, as if he were under water. He prided himself on solving problems, on rolling with life's punches. But this new situation with Olivia had left him feeling battered and weak in both mind and body.

"Is there a reason you came out?" Ronica asked, setting a cup of tea in front of him as she had so often in the past—herbal tea because too much caffeine had agitated Fletcher, and this had become their habit.

He had to consider her words several times before he could respond. "I-I don't know. Not really. I guess I was on autopilot."

She slid into the seat opposite him, not next to him, and he was both glad and saddened. Now, finally, when she was free to touch him, he was out of reach.

"I still want her to sign the papers," he admitted, fingering his cup and watching the liquid send up swirls of steam.

She snorted. "That would require selflessness and trust, both of which we know Olivia doesn't possess. I know it's a terrible situation, but I also know you don't have any choice. Not really. But no matter what, you are not doing this alone. Natalie and I went to see Olivia today, and I'm going to take her to her next appointment in Lincoln on Friday."

He lifted his head and stared. "What?"

"You heard me. You aren't doing it alone." Ronica's eyes, set in her oval face, were determined.

For a long moment, he couldn't speak. He could only stare and think about how much he loved the fire in those blue eyes and the way her short brown hair, reaching past her chin, had a slight curl, as if hinting at the passion he knew was in her soul. She was strong enough to mend a fence, set up a stage, and milk a cow, yet slender enough to make him feel strong and protective. Compared to Olivia, she was what people might call down-to-earth. But despite his family's wealth, Josiah had been raised as a simple cattle rancher, and Ronica was beautiful to him in a way Olivia had never been.

Olivia always wore layers of expensive makeup that somehow ended up looking like she wore almost none. One of her outfits likely cost more than Ronica spent in an entire year. And she either always wore a wig or had her hair weaved. In seventeen years of marriage, he'd seen her natural hair only a handful of times, and those times had mostly been in the beginning when she had loved him enough to let him glimpse her without makeup or pretense. Now those had become a shield against him. But she was definitely the perfect politician's wife, and even now thinking about her contributions to his career made him regret that he'd never been able to make her happy.

"You don't need to drive Olivia," he pulled himself together enough to say. Olivia was never kind to Ronica behind her back, and he couldn't imagine that she'd be nicer now. "I can handle it. Or pay someone."

Ronica set her cup down so hard on the table that a little tea spilled over. "You don't have a choice. We're helping. It's not up to you. And I know you're hurting and wishing it hadn't happened, but I also know you feel responsible for her, and not just because of Charlie but because you promised to take care of her in sickness and in health. I may think she's the most selfish person in the world to change tactics now when it benefits her, but I know there's nothing you can do about it except help her. And that means we're helping her too."

"Help her die, you mean." The words curdled his stomach because while he no longer loved Olivia, he had no wish for her to die.

"Or live. Miracles do happen."

He attempted a smile that felt more like a grimace. "Except when they don't."

She sighed and picked up her cup again. "Right. Before anything else, I'm your friend. I'll be here for you as you were for me and Fletcher."

"It isn't fair." He would never confess the words to anyone except her. He was the mayor, the man who always had to be positive, encouraging, and hopeful. Only with Ronica could he show any weakness because she believed in him no matter what and understood that he would eventually pick himself up and go on, just as he had years ago when Olivia had fallen out of love with him and moved on.

"No, it isn't fair." Ronica held his gaze, and it comforted him. How was it possible to still see his future in her eyes when he'd never really let himself dream of holding and loving her?

"I welcome your help," he said, "but I don't understand it. I was friends with Fletcher before he became ill, and he was a man I greatly admired. But you and Olivia?" He shook his head. "You're like fire and ice."

Ronica smiled. "She'd better be the ice."

He laughed despite himself. "Definitely."

She took a sip and lowered her cup, this time without spilling. "You said to me at the funeral that you were never letting go."

"I meant it."

"Well, now it's my turn. I'm not letting go, either, Josiah. I know you have to do this—for Charlie if for no one else—and I will be here for as long as you need me."

Her words made him want to weep with relief, but the man in him knew it was too much to ask. "It could be years. You can't put your life on hold like that."

"We're still young, and I'm a responsible adult. I can do what I want." She frowned thoughtfully. "But maybe . . . did you ever think that maybe this might be what repairs your marriage?" She said the words casually, but because he knew her heart, he recognized they hadn't come easily.

"What? No!"

Her gaze didn't waver. "Don't look at me as if I have two heads. Your heart is broken, and I know you don't want to think about it—and I don't want to think about it—but maybe this is exactly the refiner's fire Olivia needs."

"There's nothing left to repair," he said through teeth that were gritted, not from anger but from pain.

"You have every right to feel that way." She gave him a smile, but the sadness in her eyes told him she was doubtful, and that hurt him more than anything else. Yet in a way, he deserved it because he'd let her trust him and a possible future that he'd never been in a position to offer her.

"I'm sorry," he said simply.

"I know. Me too. Now drink your tea, and let's talk about moving your things back to your house."

He shook his head. "I've got a couple of suitcases in the car, and that's all I need for now. The new furnishings will remain at the mayoral residence. And I'm not even taking all my clothes.

I'm guessing I'll still go there when . . ." When Olivia became too much. When he and Charlie needed to be alone. When he needed to mourn what might have been with Ronica.

Ronica gave him a crooked smile that for the first time hinted at real amusement. "Okay, keep your man cave," she said. "But you still aren't doing this alone."

"Thank you."

Ronica watched Josiah pull out of her driveway, her heart aching more than it had since she realized what Fletcher's diagnosis meant to their future. Josiah was happier than when he arrived, but he still walked with a heaviness she could plainly see. Or maybe resolute was a better description than "happier."

Maybe happiness was out of reach for both of them.

To her surprise, Jeremy's truck was coming down the road that led to her driveway, passing Josiah's car with a brief pause as they presumably waved. Jeremy's truck stopped at the end of the drive without pulling in, and he climbed out. Before he'd reached her, his truck had continued on.

"Is that Laina driving?" she asked as he jogged toward her on the porch. "Isn't she supposed to be working? Wait, did you ask her?"

Jeremy didn't answer but looked back at where Josiah's car had vanished onto the main road. "It's spreading through town that Josiah is getting back with Olivia. What's going on? He'd never do that. Not after everything she's done. This has to be a mistake."

Ronica had guessed that everyone in Forgotten would know about their mayor's personal life by the end of the week. "So that's why Laina didn't want to come in."

"She doesn't want to pry."

Ronica nodded, grateful for Laina's courtesy. "It's not what you think. Olivia has brain cancer, and it's terminal. Or at least that's what she told Josiah." For the first time she wondered if maybe it wasn't true. Josiah would have at least seen the written diagnosis, but had that included the prognosis as well?

"Cancer? I can't believe it." Jeremy raked his hand through his hair, glancing across the snowy field to his house where Laina had parked his truck. "Poor Josiah."

"Yeah. Olivia won't sign the last addendum after all. He could fight her, but then—" She shrugged.

"But then he'd look like a jerk." He shook his head. "We're all smarter than that. Everyone knows about Olivia."

"We can't just say it's not sad because it's her," Ronica insisted.

Jeremy's lips pursed. "It's not fair."

She laughed. "So I've been told."

"I thought you and Josiah might, you know."

Ronica's heart hurt hearing it aloud. "I know, but I've just lost your dad, and maybe . . . maybe it's for the best." She didn't really feel that way because Fletcher hadn't been a partner in a very long time, but to anyone not living their lives, moving on quickly might seem disrespectful.

She pushed the thoughts away. "Anyway, what about you? What happened with Laina? Why isn't she at work? Are you taking her to the theater?"

Jeremy's grin blotted out his worry, for which Ronica was glad. He reached for her hand. "So many questions. Come on. Let's go talk to Laina."

Ronica's grin widened, and a slice of happiness pushed out the hurt in her heart. "Okay, but I'm going to need my boots." She tugged them on, and he took her hand, pulling her laughing across the snow as he had when he was a child, anxious to make snow angels. She loved that memory, and it filled her with light and love.

What he and Laina told her at his house was even better. "That's wonderful," she crowed. "A Valentine's wedding!"

"Her idea," Jeremy was quick to say.

"An amazing one!" She hugged Laina. "I'm so happy. I couldn't be happier than if you were my own daughter."

"Me too." Laina's wide grin matched Ronica's own.

"Whatever you want me to help with for your wedding, just ask. But be sure to tell me if I'm going overboard."

"It's less than a month away, so I'll need every bit of help I can get. We wanted to hold it in the reception area at City Hall, and if that's not available, we'll ask Maggie to reserve the Butter Cake."

"City Hall would be perfect!"

"My colors are going to be red and pink, and maybe a tiny bit of white. I thought maybe you could be in charge of the décor, Mom could do the food, and I'd worry about my dress and the brides-maid dresses and flowers."

"Are you sure?" Ronica asked. "I mean, I'm happy to do it, and I'm assuming we'll have a few lengthy discussions about exactly how you envision it, but I don't want to step on any toes."

"Are you kidding? You're amazing at planning, and Mom and I both agree that we don't want to do any of it without you. In fact, we had an idea about the cake." She glanced over at Jeremy and then back again at Ronica, grinning. "Jeremy said you once made a dirt cake for Fletcher that represented the farm with little bridges to other cakes and little edible animals and fields with growing veggies, and we'd like you to make one for us, if you're willing. So, a cake in the middle with connecting ones that we'll serve the guests. Mom suggested that you could even represent our store, and maybe a few other Forgotten landmarks like the reservoir."

Ronica couldn't help but feel pleased. With her other daugh-ters-in-law, she'd only been involved in paying for the rehearsal dinners, and while she'd expected to be more involved in Laina and Jeremy's wedding because it was local and she knew the Cox family so well, she hadn't expected the honor of both making the cake and decorating the venue.

She fought back tears. "I could do that. In fact, the main cake could represent your house and the farm, with the grain silo being the part that you freeze for your first anniversary. I'll add extra layers of chocolate cake and something around it to hold the shape, though. Regular dirt cake won't hold form that high."

"I love that idea." Laina clapped her hands, flushing with excitement.

"The good news is that the Valentine's Dance at the high school is actually being held the Friday before Valentine's, so there will be no competing town event that day. It falls on a Tuesday this year, but that's okay since everyone will come because they'll want to celebrate on the day itself."

Jeremy snorted. "Give out free food, and just about anyone in town will come."

"It'll be a dinner then?"

Laina nodded. "I'm the last kid to marry, and my parents are more than excited. They thought I was going to be an old maid."

Jeremy pulled her close. "Never. I know how you have to fend them off, but I promise, I'm the man for you."

"I know." They began kissing.

Ronica laughed and averted her gaze, even though the sight filled her with joy. "Okay, you two. I'm going to let you celebrate. But I'm making cake if you want to come over later."

"I need to get back to the store, but I'll be by tonight," Laina broke away from Jeremy long enough to say.

"I'll double the recipe then," Ronica said, half to herself. "That way I can practice for the wedding cake and still have one to take to Olivia tonight."

Jeremy and Laina stopped kissing to stare at her. "Olivia?" Jeremy asked with a touch of disbelief.

Ronica forced a smile. "Yes, Olivia. She's craving my cake."

Jeremy looked at Laina and then back at her. "Can I tell her?"

"Of course. Everyone will know soon enough." At the moment,

only she and Natalie knew about the cancer, but that too would come out—and the sooner the better. That way none of Josiah's defenders would think less of him for sticking with a woman who had not only cheated on him but tried to take everything he'd ever worked for. Even as the thought came, she realized what an impossible situation he was in. Some people would judge him no matter what choice he made.

"Well, that explains a lot," Laina said after Jeremy told her about the cancer. "I'm sorry."

"Me too. But we'll all help." Ronica took a breath. "But this means I'll be going to Lincoln on Friday if you want a ride. They have some nice wedding dress stores there."

Laina looked at her doubtfully. "Somehow I don't see Olivia enjoying our company."

"Maybe not," Ronica said. "But it's not all up to her now, is it?"

Laina grinned. "I guess not. I'll talk to my mom and see what we can pull together. The sooner we get the dress the better."

Ronica hurried back to her house, thinking of ways to make an impressive cake that both looked and tasted great. She'd have to incorporate a lot of different ideas, so it would no longer really be a dirt cake, but that was okay. And she'd probably need to get Maggie from the café onboard. She was a master at making food actually taste as good as it looked.

Ronica skipped dinner and went right to making the cake. There was only one incident of shock when she turned to ask Fletcher if he wanted to lick the pudding bowl, and of course he wasn't there. As she stared at the empty chair, all the emotions of the day rushed through her. She collapsed to the table and cried with deep convulsive sobs. She cried for Fletcher, for herself, for Josiah, for Charlie, and even for Olivia.

And just like that, she was back to playing the what-if game. What if she'd met Josiah before marrying Fletcher? What would her life be like at this moment? Would they be happy? Would Ronica give up the joy and love she had experienced to avoid the ending pain and possibly have a better overall life? Then again, what if she had married Josiah and their lives turned out worse because neither had yet learned the lessons that made them so compatible today?

There were no answers. There was no time machine. The only choice was to go forward.

She got up, splashed water on her face, and went back to work. But instead of coming up with a farmhouse and silo arrangement for the cake, she came up with something that vaguely resembled historic City Hall, which told her she was still thinking of Josiah.

No good. She needed to find a way to go on without the hope of him in her future.

CHAPTER 10

Early Friday morning, the freezing air stung Ronica's lungs as she tromped over the shoveled walk in the semi-darkness to Olivia's mansion. It was colder here by the lake—she would almost swear to it. Olivia answered the door herself after only a few seconds, her tall figure looking elegant and willowy in a black suit and long coat. Pearls stood out notably on ebony skin. Today her hair was a straight, gorgeous, medium brown that reached past her shoulders.

"Ready?" Ronica asked brightly. "We've got snacks!"

Olivia looked past Ronica to the pink Volkswagen Beetle in Olivia's driveway, where Laina awaited them. "I am not driving to Lincoln in that thing," she announced.

"What?" Ronica was confused. "I knew you wouldn't want me to drive my silver truck—Jeremy calls her Crank these days for a reason—but Laina's car is nice, if a little bright." She grinned, hesitating. "We knew it would be too loud for us to go in Pamela's van with the rest of the wedding dress shoppers, and besides, not everyone would fit, so Laina offered to drive us more comfortably than in my truck. And don't worry. They're staying in a different unit from us at my son's rental, so you'll have all the privacy—"

"It's not that," Olivia said, lifting her chin a little in challenge. "I may need to recline on the way home, and there won't be space in that little . . . tin can. We'll take my car."

"But . . . do you think you'll be able to drive?"

"You can drive it. Or I guess Laina." She gave a long-suffering sigh. "You can use my car after you drop me off at the cancer center too."

"Someone is going to stay with you."

"Please." Olivia gave her a flat smile. "You don't want to do this anymore than I want you to. I know you are all doing this for me because you care about Josiah wearing himself out. But it's your son's wedding, and you should be there with Laina. I'm not going to be the reason you miss that." Her expression became almost angry. "I wouldn't miss it for you if Charlie were getting married." With that, she whirled and started to slam the door.

Ronica put her foot out to stop it from shutting. "I won't miss anything because Natalie will be there too. We're stopping to pick her up, and we're planning on taking turns staying with you throughout the whole trip."

Olivia didn't look back at her, but Ronica could see the side of her face where a tear cascaded down her cheek. "Okay," she said softly. "I'll meet you outside."

This time Ronica let her shut the door. Poor Olivia. Ronica should have known better than to mention the wedding when Olivia likely wouldn't be around for Charlie's.

Laina jumped out of her car, rubbing her arms against the cold. "Is she not going?"

"She wants to take her car."

"That new Lexus SUV she's been driving around? Cool. Do you think she'll let me take it for a spin?"

"Yes, but maybe I should take the first leg. And when you do drive, maybe you can—"

"Go slow?" Laina laughed. "I know. I know. I have a lead foot. I promise to drive slowly—at least if she's in the car. Have to admit I really like the idea of showing up to the wedding shops in a fancy Lexus. I am still dropping you off, right, and then coming back after we have brunch but before we go to the first shop?"

"Yep. Plans are the same. But I'll take an Uber and meet you."

The double garage door in front of them opened, and for a moment Ronica thought Laina might have to move the Beetle, but the garage itself was more than two cars deep, giving Olivia enough room to angle her gunmetal gray Lexus out and around Laina's car. Josiah's car was nowhere to be seen, and Ronica found herself wondering where he might be. Charlie would need to be at school soon, though maybe he'd had an early project.

Before Ronica could warn Laina not to talk about the wedding, Laina grabbed her large duffle bag and jumped in the back seat. More slowly, Ronica transferred her own bag and a cooler from the Beetle to the Lexus as Olivia climbed out and went around to the front passenger seat, inclining the seat and uttering a sigh.

Ronica exchanged an uncertain glance with Laina before carefully backing out of the drive. She couldn't believe how smoothly the car drove. Maybe Olivia had the right idea.

They hadn't even reached Natalie's when Laina pulled out full-color brochures and wedding magazines. "I can't decide between a mermaid or princess style like the dress Keisha bought. I know it's silly, but I always wanted to look like a princess, although I'm so short that I'm worried it's going to make me look like a chubby ball of puff. Anyway, here are my favorites. What do you think, Olivia?" She shoved the papers through the large opening between the front bucket seats in Olivia's direction.

"Huh?" Olivia's eyes blinked open.

"I've marked my favorites. What do you think? I know you're familiar with all the latest trends, but it's not so much trends I care about but rather knocking Jeremy's socks off when I walk into the room, you know?"

Olivia actually smiled. "Yes. Let's see." She thumbed through the papers.

Ronica hoped Laina was ready to have her dreams crushed, but at least Olivia hadn't already wadded the images up and tossed them back. As for Laina's feelings, Ronica couldn't really do anything about that now as she'd pulled up to Natalie's, and the honk didn't bring her out.

"I'll go grab her." She left the car running and hurried through the snow on the driveway.

She'd scheduled plenty of leeway to get everyone where they needed to go on time, but Natalie had been rather emotional last night when they'd talked on the phone—not that Ronica could blame her. Her friend was going through a lot.

Natalie came from the house before she reached the porch. She handed Ronica a cooler before reaching down for an overnight case. "I'm about running on no sleep because of social media," she said brightly, "but thank you for finding that Facebook group for me. I never realized so many parents out there were estranged from their adult children. It's awful, but at the same time, it's so great to know I'm not alone, that I'm not crazy or deserving of all this hatred Joni is sending my way."

"I could have told you that," Ronica said. "In fact, I think I did."

Natalie chuckled. "You did. Anyway, are you sure it'll be okay for me to go meet the people I've connected with in Lincoln? I know I shouldn't have tried to sneak that in on this trip, but it's one thing to read what they write and another to meet them in person. I guess I just need proof that we aren't the monsters our children want us to believe we are."

Ronica gave her a one-armed hug. "You aren't. I know that very well. And you have nothing to be ashamed of. There will be plenty of time for you to visit. I'll sit with Olivia tonight at the rental. The bridal shops will be closed by then."

"Thank you." Tears shone in Natalie's eyes, but they made it to the Lexus without any falling. "Wow," she muttered, eyeing the SUV. "I didn't know we'd be going in this kind of style. I might have dressed up more."

"You are dressed up," Ronica guessed, though she couldn't see her friend's clothing well under her coat. But between Olivia and the other women she planned to meet, she'd be looking her best. Ronica herself was wearing gray dress pants that were loose enough to be comfortable but were definitely not her favorite jeans.

Back in the SUV, the air felt hot, and she realized Olivia must have turned the heat on full blast. She shrugged out of her coat before putting the car in gear.

"I know the princess look is appealing, but it's only for women with rather large busts and small hips," Olivia was saying, leaning on her elbow as she turned to speak with Laina in the back seat. "As I've been saying, the A-line or a mermaid could work, but I suspect that a trumpet style, fitted on top with a deep V in front like this one, will not only make you appear taller but will also give you a bit of the fullness you want, though only at the bottom." Olivia drew invisible lines on the paper with her finger, her brow scrunched in concentration. "If you choose a fit and flare dress where the flare begins just below the hips but has more flow than fullness, that might even be better. I don't see an example here, but the ladies at the store will know what you mean if you ask." She handed back the papers, then laid her head against the leather headrest as if the effort of speaking had drained her.

The dress Olivia chose wasn't one Laina had even circled. Ronica gave Laina a shrug, but the young woman only grinned back. "Thanks, Olivia," she said brightly. "I'll give it a try."

"Ooh, let me see." Natalie was all over the papers with the

eagerness of a woman who had two adult daughters and no wedding in sight. "And I'm sorry we don't have more time, Laina, or I would make you one of these at half the cost. But with what I've already scheduled, there's no way I could do it justice, even if we could get our hands on a good design and the right material."

"It's my fault for wanting to get married so quickly." Laina waved her hand, dismissing Natalie's concerns. "I'm just glad to have your opinion. What do you think?"

The drive to Lincoln might have been tedious, but the Lexus made the trip a pure joy. It didn't feel like an SUV at all, and the way it hugged the curves and made seventy feel more like forty had Ronica envious. It was time for a new car. Maybe not one like this, but the truck . . . that was Fletcher's. Not really hers. Why had she never bought a new one?

With a sudden wave of guilt, she realized she hadn't thought of Fletcher all morning. Or most of yesterday, as she'd been so busy with wedding plans. Fletcher would be happy for her. Tomorrow would be a week since his death. Why did it suddenly feel like a year?

There was a hole in her heart, however, one that had been filled with Josiah's daily visits to check in with Fletcher. She hadn't seen him since Monday night when she'd taken the dirt cake to Olivia. She'd tried to make it look like City Hall, and Josiah had seen her attempt for what it was right away, though Olivia looked skeptical. They'd invited her to stay for a piece, but she'd begged off, citing Laina and Jeremy's pending visit. But the real truth, that she admitted only to herself, was she simply couldn't bear to see Olivia acting as if she and Josiah were a normal, loving couple when his hurt was so clearly written on his face.

Could Olivia see it? Did she even care?

As she'd walked to her truck after leaving the cake, Charlie had burst from the house to talk to her. "Thanks for the cake!" he said. "It's my favorite."

"Any time," she said wholeheartedly. "I'm willing to make it or anything else for you whenever you want. You hear? Just give me a call."

He nodded, but he didn't lope off with a shy smile as he normally did. "Ms. Ronica," he started, though she'd asked him many times to drop the Ms. "Uh, you know about my mom, right?"

"Yes. And I'm very sorry."

"Thank you. But it's really my dad I'm worried about. He's . . . he's not himself. It feels like . . . like he's gone."

She dropped her hand from her truck door, facing him completely. "Sometimes it takes a while for things this hard to settle. Don't worry. Your dad's not going anywhere, and he'll be okay. Just give him a little time."

"Okay. I will. Thank you." At last, the anticipated smile appeared on his rounded face before he turned away.

Ronica still hadn't talked to Josiah about the incident. It wasn't something she could address in a text message or even on the phone, mostly because talking to Josiah and shaking him from wherever he'd gone without betraying Charlie's confidence was a fine line to walk. After today, she'd figure it out.

At the cancer center, Laina took over the wheel of the Lexus, her excitement radiating through her eyes. Ronica was glad that Olivia and Natalie were inside the door before Laina sped away.

Ronica followed them inside to see Olivia moving slowly through the lobby as if her muscles had solidified during the drive. At forty-six, Olivia shouldn't be moving like that, but then cancer changed everything, and she was already taking chemo drugs, which meant high doses to pass the blood-brain barrier or something, as Laina had explained on their way to Olivia's that morning after watching a video about it on YouTube.

Natalie dropped back to stand with Ronica, letting Olivia approach the receptionist alone. "You should have gone with Laina," she whispered.

"I'll stay for a bit. This has got to be tough."

Thirty minutes early for the appointment, they were directed to a room to wait. Olivia was looking fainter by the moment, so Ronica and Natalie kept up a running dialogue about the construction progress on the new pasta factory and how the police had given double the traffic citations since the construction workers came to town.

"It's like they can't seem to understand that we still have speed limits, even if we only have one traffic light." Natalie rolled her eyes.

"The proceeds are good for the town, though," Ronica said. "And they're spending money. I wonder how many will end up staying."

"Not many, I don't think," Natalie said. "It's the new workers that'll inhabit those new little box houses that will increase our population."

"Is it just me, or do they all look alike?" Ronica mused. "The houses, not the construction workers."

Their conversation seemed to alternately disgust or amuse Olivia, which was the intent after all. At long last, the doctors came to get Olivia to take her back for the radiation.

"Go now," Natalie urged once she'd left the room.

Ronica narrowed her eyes. "You're not going to leave her, are you?"

Natalie groaned. "Don't tempt me. But no." She pulled out her phone. "I'm just going to read the new posts on that estranged parent group. I know it's almost macabre, but it gives me a deep comfort to know that so many other parents are going through this. It's like an entire generation, you know? And most parents are as confused as I am as to why our grown kids can't just tell us what they need instead of blocking and hiding."

"I'm glad it's helping you." Maybe that was what Natalie needed—to grieve so she could find happiness again. "Look, when you guys get finished here, text me. I'll grab the car and take you back to the apartment. Olivia will need to rest, and I don't know what food she'll be able to eat. She may feel nauseated."

"No doubt. She's obviously lost weight. We're staying at your son's place, right? Where we stayed for our Christmas shopping trip?"

"Yeah. We have one side of the four-plex. Two units."

"Then once we get there, I'll go out to that little grocery shop we found around the corner and grab some things. I should be able to find something to tempt Olivia. If not, we can order in."

"Sounds like a plan."

Ronica left Natalie scrolling intently on her phone. She hoped she hadn't made the situation ultimately worse for her friend by finding the group, but how could having people understand what you were going through be a bad thing? A similar group had helped her come to terms with the pending loss of her husband, and though she'd only stayed in the group for a year, there had been many sleepless nights when complete strangers had been her only support—mostly because she didn't like to show weakness in front of her friends and family. But maybe not wanting to share was a weakness.

She smiled and thought about texting the idea to Josiah, as she once would have done without hesitation, but she didn't this time. It felt wrong somehow, though she knew nothing had changed between him and Olivia.

And yet everything else had changed.

In Ronica's mind, pity vied with irritation toward Olivia. Life was like that. *I can hold on,* she thought. But the idea of what that meant was obscure to her at the moment, which was perhaps a blessing in disguise. Ronica wasn't the same person she had been five years ago. Would Josiah also change with Olivia's illness? It was entirely likely.

She took an Uber to join Laina's group at their first stop only two blocks away, which Laina had planned to help Ronica catch up to them. She was as good at planning as Ronica, and she could envision passing the Ladies Auxiliary presidency to her someday. Right now the fifty-something women took turns, but some of them were growing weary of taking care of abandoned homes, making sure the calling tree went smoothly, and being awakened in the middle of the night for emergencies. Ronica knew she was tired, though she still loved planning the town events.

Laina was in the dressing room with her mother, Pamela, when Ronica arrived. Both Laina's grandmothers; her sister, Trish Baker; her pregnant sister-in-law, Cheyenne Cox; and Laina's friends Keisha Jefferson and Ayleen Jenkins were scattered on chairs in front of a wall of mirrors.

"What did I miss?" Ronica asked.

Trish snorted. "Only a princess dress from Butter Ball City. She literally looked like a round ball."

"No way." Ronica couldn't believe that. "I mean, her waist is so slim."

Keisha, who was Olivia's niece through her deceased half brother, put her phone in front of Ronica's face. "Believe it. The dress was beautiful, but it didn't do Laina any favors."

Ronica stared at the picture, wincing internally. "Oh, yeah. That's too bad. To be fair, Olivia did say it wouldn't look good."

Keisha laughed. "Well, if there is one thing my aunt knows, it's what will look good. Remember how she knew which dress was going to look fantastic on me and how she twisted my arm to get me to try it on?"

"We remember." Cheyenne tossed a length of her dark hair over her shoulder as she leaned back in her chair. "I confess I was in shock that she was even shopping with you after what she did to you and Xander."

"I know." Keisha shrugged. "But she is my only female relative. Thankfully, Maggie and Laina were there to buffer her." She looked down, her curly brown hair covering her olive skin and hazel eyes. "I feel so bad even saying that with her diagnosis."

No one said anything for several seconds, and then Ronica asked, "Where is Maggie anyway? I thought she was coming."

Keisha shook her head. "We're too short at the café, as usual, so it was either her or me. Anyway, the van only had seven seats, so we'd have had to crowd Olivia. We didn't know you'd be taking her car instead of Laina's little Bug—that was going to be a tight fit with the four of you. But we'll keep video-chatting with Maggie as Laina comes out in the dresses." A smile stretched across her face. "You should have seen Maggie's face when I showed her the butter ball dress." All the ladies chuckled, even the grandmothers, Judith Cox and Sable Lewis, who had been intent on their own conversation.

"So if you got a dress, when are you getting married?" Judith asked Keisha. "I didn't miss it, did I?"

More laughter. "No," Keisha replied. "I was thinking in April so we can go to a sunny beach in Florida for our honeymoon. I don't know who's more annoyed, my aunt at me for not giving her a date, or Xander for not eloping three months ago."

"Will Olivia be . . . uh, around then?" Cheyenne asked, standing to stretch her rounded stomach. She was five months along but looked ready to run a marathon.

"Well, that's why she's getting treatment, right?" Ronica said. "To make a few more milestones."

Keisha grimaced. "I may have to change my plans."

"Way to kill the mood, Cheyenne," Ayleen said from her own seat next to the grandmothers. As usual, her dishwater blond hair was up in its fine ponytail, and she wore no makeup. Her teeth when she smiled were white and perfectly even, changing her from ordinary to pretty.

"Look, there she is." Keisha pointed toward the dressing room.

Ronica looked up to see Laina in a satin dress that was beaded and fitted on top, flaring out loosely starting at the thigh, growing to full and flowing at the bottom and extending in an amazing train. If not appearing taller, Laina certainly didn't look short—or remotely like a ball of butter.

"Oh, wow," Ronica said at the same time Ayleen whistled. "What's that one?" Ronica asked.

"It's called a trumpet," Keisha said.

The style Olivia recommended, Ronica thought. She looked at one of the store employees. "Do you have any fit and flare dresses that look like this?" What was it Olivia had said? "Where maybe the flare begins right around or below her hips?"

"Yes. And I think I have just the one." The woman smiled. "It'll give the princess feel she wants but without the bulk on the hips."

Laina spun on a pedestal in front of the mirrors. "I don't know. This one is pretty perfect. Would it be wrong of me to want to stop now?"

Her mother laughed. "Ah, give me a few more dresses, sweetie. I'm sure enjoying seeing you out of your jeans and tool belt." Everyone laughed at that.

After three more dresses that no one liked, the second employee finally returned with a dress that was eighty percent lace, with a lovely V-neck that fitted tightly along Laina's torso until it flared out, higher in the back and lower on the sides at the hips, into an amazingly full and flowing train. The dress was too large in the shoulders, but with a little pinning, it would fit Laina like a glove.

"This is it," Laina breathed out the words.

"Dang right." Keisha pumped her fist in the air.

"Yes!" Trish and Cheyenne gave Laina the thumbs up and dived in for some pictures.

"What about the other two stores?" Ronica said.

"They were only backups," Laina said. "You know how I hate shopping."

"The price?" Ayleen asked.

Smiles faded, as everyone turned to look at the employees. Laina gasped when they told her. "We'll leave you to talk about it," one said.

"That's double our budget," Laina murmured to her mother, "and it's a generous budget."

"Too bad there's no time to order one from China," Ayleen offered. "That's what my cousin did. Her dress was a fourth of the price. She had to pay fifty bucks to a local lady for tailoring, though."

"If I had that kind of time, I would've asked Natalie to make my dress." Laina looked at her mother. "I really want this dress, but I don't want you to spend more. Do you think I should pay in installments? Or should I find something for less? That other dress was good, right?"

"You might be able to rent one," Trish said with a sigh. "But I love owning my dress."

"I'll talk to your father." Pamela fingered the dress, a slight twist to her lips. "But maybe we should go check out those other stores."

Ronica was beginning to feel guilty for asking them to find the dress. She was about to volunteer to pitch in when Judith stood and took her granddaughter's hands. "You're so beautiful, Laina. This is the dress, and Sable and I want to buy it for you."

"Oh, no. I couldn't accept." Laina flushed a deep red as she always did when embarrassed or troubled.

"We insist." Judith took Laina's hands. "You are our last grand-daughter, and we aren't getting any younger."

Sable took one of Laina's hands from Judith. "That's right. We can't take it with us, dear." She laughed. "Besides, you make us proud in that dress. You are certainly carrying on our family tradition of extraordinary brides. No one is ever going to forget you in that. Especially Jeremy."

Tears stung Ronica's eyes as she thought about the connections of family. Her parents had been long gone by the time her children were teenagers, and the same with Fletcher's, but this was the kind of grandmother she hoped to be to her grandchildren.

Laina hugged first one grandmother and then the other. "Thank you so much! I can't say that I don't feel a little frivolous, but I really do want this dress. I can't wait for Jeremy to see me in it."

After that, there was more pinning and tucking, followed by Judith and Sable counting out money in bills of all sizes onto the counter. They'd obviously come prepared with the intention of helping Laina.

Afterward, they migrated to a nearby mall, where they found a café that sold specialty chocolates and laughed themselves silly. Feeling guilty for enjoying herself while Natalie was stuck at the cancer center, Ronica texted her for the fifth time.

I can come now. She bought that last dress I sent you a picture of. We're having some chocolates now. I bought you a few.

Yummy. Thanks. And okay. But we're actually not at the cancer center anymore. Once you left, it literally took only an hour. Olivia was feeling good, so we decided to go to Nordstrom. We used an Uber (yes, a fancy one) because we didn't want you to miss the dress shopping.

Wow, okay. Thanks.

Nothing like some good shopping therapy! She's flagging fast, though, so I maybe shouldn't have encouraged it.

No, it's good for her to get out. And thank you for staying with her. I'll come get you now.

Ronica put away her phone and announced to the ladies, "Believe it or not, Olivia and Natalie are at Nordstrom."

"I believe it," Keisha said. "It's one of her favorites."

"Who wants to come pick them up with me?" Ronica asked as Laina gave her the keys to the Lexus. "You won't have enough seats to get back to the rental apartment in Pamela's van."

"I will." Keisha jumped up from the small table, grabbing a small bag of chocolates she'd bought to take home. "I'd like to see how my aunt is doing."

"Okay," Laina said. "But don't forget we're going out to eat tonight, even if we have to take two cars."

"I won't." Keisha gave everyone a wave and walked out with Ronica. "So about the radiation. Did Natalie say anything?"

"Not really. I wonder how long it takes to get the results."

Keisha shrugged, her face hopeful. "I understood that they'd be doing some post examination today since this was supposed to be so intensive. Maybe shopping was her way of celebrating."

Dread wielded its ugly head inside Ronica's chest. If Olivia's procedure today had gone well, would that mean she'd soon feel healthy enough to let Josiah go, or would it only mean more years of using him? Or maybe winning him back? And if the tumor didn't shrink, would being glad for Josiah's sake be a crime? Because if Olivia was no longer around to use him, he'd be free.

Maybe it wasn't dread in her heart but envy or something much worse.

Either way, she'd lost Josiah. Maybe forever. Because life kept throwing curveballs, so if there was something she didn't expect, it was probably the thing that would most likely happen.

The old familiar stab of pain shot through her heart, but this time it wasn't from losing Fletcher. It was for losing Josiah.

For a second time.

CHAPTER 11

Outside, huge snowflakes fell from the sky, gathering slowly on the sidewalks on top of older snow. They were the big, fat snowflakes that stuck to your lashes and left wet patches on your skin when they melted. Ronica lifted her face to the sky.

"What are you doing?" Keisha asked.

"I don't know." Ronica laughed, a little embarrassed. "Just saying hello, I guess. This is my favorite kind of snow. It means it's warming up. Mark my words, we'll have things melting a bit again over the next few days. At least that's what Fletcher always said when this kind started falling."

Keisha smiled, catching flakes and rubbing her hands together. "Fletcher was always right." She waited until they were in the car to ask, "Do you miss him?"

Ronica took a deep breath before answering. "So much that it still feels like a knife to the chest sometimes, but it's the old Fletcher I miss, not what he became."

"I liked it when you'd bring him to the Butter Cake. He was mostly super sweet."

Ronica smiled. "Yes. Little boy sweet. It was so . . . odd . . . and confusing. On some level I miss that too, but mostly I'm just happy he's no longer dealing with all the issues that came with his dementia, both physical and mental."

Keisha nodded, and the conversation moved back to Laina's dress and Keisha's own upcoming nuptials. When the conversation turned to Olivia, the younger woman frowned. "What if my aunt doesn't make it until April? Three months ago, I wouldn't have cared at all if she missed my wedding, but now . . . now I feel like I should do everything I can to include her. It's like everything she did wrong really doesn't matter anymore."

"It matters," Ronica said, pulling into a parking spot near Nordstrom. "But death has a way of bringing the most important things to the foreground. And forgiveness is always, always the best road to travel."

Keisha started to open the door, then stopped. "I don't know that I would be so charitable if I were you. Not giving my uncle a divorce just because she's going to die is . . . Well, it seems she hasn't learned a thing about using and controlling people. I think she gave up every right to have my uncle in her life. And for him, being with her isn't any way to live." Keisha's gaze pinned Ronica in place. "I wish you'd convince him not to do what she's asking."

Ronica pondered that for several moments. "I don't think he has any choice. Not really. It's who he is." Josiah was honorable, perhaps even to a fault. For example, he hadn't once been inappropriate with her, though sometimes she'd almost wanted him to be. Nothing major, of course, because of her loyalty to Fletcher, but maybe to tell her everything in his heart, or to simply reach out and hold her hand.

"Yeah, maybe you're right." Keisha sighed and pushed her door open.

Inside Nordstrom, Olivia and Natalie were seated near the door on a wooden bench. Natalie was on her phone while Olivia huddled in her coat, looking exhausted. Guilt spread through Ronica, and she forced cheeriness into her words. "Hope you bought something fun," she said, eyeing the two large bags near their feet.

"We did." Olivia's voice was clipped. Then her expression softened as her gaze shifted to Keisha. "I didn't know you were coming."

"I couldn't miss seeing Laina find the perfect wedding dress." Keisha sat down next to her.

Olivia's shoulders curled in a bit more. "I guess not."

Had Olivia thought Keisha had come for her? After keeping Keisha and Xander apart for years with her prejudice, how could she possibly expect that? Dying didn't magically erase the past.

The reaction wasn't lost on Keisha, but instead of calling her aunt out, she said, "Apparently, you won the prize for the best dress suggestion."

"Really?"

"Didn't Natalie show you?" Ronica asked.

"Hey, she was in the fitting room when you texted." What she didn't say, but what Ronica perceived, was that Olivia had taken a very long time in the fitting room.

Natalie switched over from Facebook to a picture of Laina and held it out for Olivia to see. "Here we go. Doesn't she look lovely?"

Olivia nodded, a tight, pleased smile coming to her lips. "I knew a trumpet style would be best. She really does look lovely."

Full stop. No exception and no further recommendation. Just a straight compliment.

Ronica purposefully didn't look at Natalie, who would have also noticed the unusually kind response. "I agree. She'll make a beautiful bride."

"What about the treatment?" Keisha asked. "How did it go?"

Olivia's lips pursed momentarily before saying, "They want me to come back in the morning for a higher concentrated dose. They didn't see the initial changes they expected today."

Keisha's face creased with concern. "I'm so sorry."

Olivia didn't answer but bent over to retrieve one of her bags. "This is for your honeymoon. Never underestimate the power of a few fantastic negligees."

"Really?" Keisha's smile widened. "Thank you so much! That's sweet."

Ronica waited for Olivia to ask about Keisha's wedding date, but Olivia simply smiled and said, "You're welcome."

Olivia reached for the other bag and rose a bit unsteadily. She was definitely moving more slowly than when they first arrived in Lincoln, and Keisha kept giving her worried glances as they trudged through the snow in the direction of the Lexus, which thankfully wasn't far.

"This will make you feel better, right?" Keisha asked. "Eventually, I mean?"

"Maybe for a while," Olivia answered, her steps pausing. "They don't really know. But right now . . ." She trailed off, sweeping a glance over all of them. "Right now I feel awful."

Keisha gave her aunt a gentle squeeze before offering her arm. "Let's get you to the apartment."

Ronica wanted to remind Keisha to be careful, that Olivia wasn't above using her illness to get what she wanted, though Keisha should already know this better than anyone else. Still, Ronica would keep an eye on the situation.

Ronica gave up her place by Olivia's side to Natalie and hurried ahead of the others to incline the front passenger seat as far as it would go. Silas's four-plex was only minutes from the shopping center, but with Olivia's tightlipped grimace, it seemed an eternity. As it was the low season, three of the four units had been available, and Silas was more than happy to let her use two of them at a steep discount, which wasn't customary of his mercenary self. Maybe the land his father had given him in his will made a difference to the problems he'd been having with Jeremy's inheritance. Ronica could only hope.

Both their assigned apartments, one upstairs and the other down, had three bedrooms with an additional couch bed in the living room, if needed. They chose the ground floor unit for Olivia, tucking her into a queen bed with fresh linens that Olivia had insisted on bringing, even though Ronica assured her the sheets were always washed before each guest.

"Nice place." Keisha scanned the room. "Better than the hotels I normally stay in, and it's got a full kitchen." To her aunt, she added, "What can I make you?"

"I feel too nauseated now to eat anything." Olivia adjusted the pillow under her head and put an arm over her eyes. "Maybe later you can make some of the oatmeal I brought."

"Oatmeal?" Keisha echoed with a frown. "I thought you hated that."

"Well, nothing tastes good anymore, so it doesn't really matter what I eat." Olivia didn't open her eyes as she spoke.

They all stared at each other for a few moments before Keisha waved them out. "I'll stay with her."

As they left the room, pulling the door mostly closed, they heard Keisha say, "Why don't we get that wig off? You'll be more comfortable. I can tie on one of your scarves." Whatever Olivia responded was soft and garbled.

Sighing, Natalie said in a soft voice, "Poor Olivia."

"She'd hate us saying that." Ronica sank to the sofa and put her feet up on the coffee table, thinking Silas wouldn't mind since she'd taken her boots off by the door.

"I know, but she's not herself." Natalie hesitated. "She saw the title of the online group I was looking at, and I told her a little. I was surprised when she didn't tell me to write Joni off immediately."

"That is something. Should we go to that little shop now?" Ronica asked. "The girls will be going out to eat, but we might as well get some snacks and something for breakfast."

"Olivia might be able to eat a smoothie," Natalie mused. "If we can find the ingredients, I can make her a fresh organic one with soy. Joni loves those when she's having problems eating." Her face suddenly went bleak.

Ronica hopped up from the couch before her friend could fall into despair. "Let's go then."

By the time they returned with groceries, Laina and her party had already arrived in the upstairs apartment and were getting ready for an early dinner. Ronica and Natalie dropped the snacks off there before going downstairs to check on Olivia.

"Will you be coming to dinner?" Laina asked her as they turned to leave.

Ronica sighed internally. "I don't think so, but I'll be up for a while later," she said, making her voice light. "After Natalie gets back from her meeting."

Laina eyed her sympathetically. "If Olivia feels up to it, she's more than welcome to come with us to dinner. I mean, dinner should be less effort than Nordstrom, right?"

Wild, crazy laughter boiled up inside Ronica because she knew not a single one of them, not even her, wanted to be around Olivia for a celebratory dinner. Ronica shook her head. "Thanks for the offer, but that's not going to be possible. She lost steam pretty fast. It's been rough." The relief in the faces around the room was nearly palpable.

"So how did the treatment go?" Laina asked.

Ronica glanced at Natalie and then back at Laina, all too aware of the other women also waiting to hear the answer. "We don't know any details, but it doesn't seem to be good news. She's going back for another dose in the morning before we leave tomorrow."

"They'll up the dose again," Natalie added. "But today was higher than the last round of treatments she had over a five-day period. It was supposed to be just the one."

Laina frowned. "That doesn't sound great. I mean, I know radiation can take time to shrink tumors, but there should be some initial change, right?"

Ronica shrugged, unable to speak past the lump in her throat. Sometimes nothing worked. She knew that all too well. "Well, we need to go check on her and give Keisha a break." She forced a brightness she didn't feel. "Who knows? Maybe Olivia is doing better, and no one will need to stay with her tonight."

In the downstairs apartment, Keisha was in the living room, sitting on the couch. She wiped a tear from her cheek as Ronica hurried toward her. "What is it? Is she okay?"

Keisha shook her head. "No, she's not." She glanced toward the closed bedroom door, lowering her voice. "She has a horrible scar on her head at the tumor site. Like a burn. Must be from the first round of radiation, but it's sore again now. I could barely get her to let me help put something on it. I had no idea. And she did all this alone the first time. Well, I guess her boyfriend hung around a few days, but then he left her in the apartment and went to stay with his parents until she finished."

"Wow," Natalie said, setting her groceries on the counter in the adjoining kitchen and joining Keisha on the couch. "That's cruel."

Keisha lifted her jaw, clenching it noticeably before saying, "That's her world. And I could absolutely see her doing that to him or to me or to my uncle. She is a firm believer in taking care of her own happiness first. I think Charlie would be the only one she might . . ." She shook her head. "I don't know how to deal with this. For a while after my parents died, she was the only reason I kept it together. But then she was so controlling, I only wanted to get away from her. And after I learned that she was responsible for ripping Xander from my life because she considered him white trash . . ." The tears fell in earnest. "I thought I'd forgiven her for all that, but I guess I'm still really angry, and I don't want to feel sorry for her."

Ronica sat on Keisha's other side, slipping an arm around her slender frame. "That's completely understandable. Absolutely. Look, wash your face and go upstairs with the others. They're getting ready to go out to dinner."

She shook her head. "No, she's my family, my responsibility. And you should be with Laina."

"There will be time enough for you to step in," Ronica told her. "You go on, and I'll join you all upstairs later."

"I won't be too late." Natalie patted Keisha's hand. "And I don't mind staying with Olivia, either. We are all in this together. Just remember that."

Keisha gave a little sigh and straightened her shoulders. "You know, when I was a kid, I hated how everyone in town seemed to know everything about everyone else, but now I see that it really does take a village. Sometimes I want more than anything to have a mother again. I know Olivia can never be that, but having all of you from the Ladies Auxiliary makes up for so much. There isn't one of you that I couldn't call for help. I'm proud to be a member."

Natalie let out a huge sniff. "Well, I find myself nearly daughterless right now with my girls so far away, so you are a blessing to me."

Keisha gave her a hug. "Thank you."

"Poor thing," Natalie murmured as Keisha left the apartment. "I can't imagine how this is affecting her. We need to make sure she has the best wedding in the world."

Ronica nodded. "Yes, but even more important, we need to make sure she doesn't get stuck under Olivia's thumb." She glanced at Olivia's door.

"Right. Good point." Natalie's face turned pensive. "It's so odd that Keisha can still love and care for Olivia after all she's done, and she still hopes to forgive her, while my daughter, who I've tried to give everything, doesn't have enough love to even try to work things out with me."

"It does seem lopsided," Ronica agreed. "Maybe it's a matter of maturity."

Natalie jumped up from the couch. "Well, I'm going to make that smoothie now before my ride gets here. The doctor told Olivia to eat regularly, and she hasn't had anything since early this morning."

"I'll go wake her up."

Olivia wasn't sleeping, though. She was lying back on a huge mound of pillows Keisha must have taken from the other rooms and closets. She looked frail but also stylish, her beige headwrap contrasting with her dark, beautiful skin.

"Natalie is making you a smoothie," Ronica announced. "It's supposed to be easy on the digestive system." Before Olivia could protest, she rushed on, "Would you like me to put something on the television for you?" She gestured to the one on the wall. Silas had balked at putting one in each bedroom, but his wife assured him the four-plex would rent faster.

"I guess." Olivia looked at her through half-closed eyes, her unnaturally thick lashes making shadows on her face. "I think I'm too exhausted to sleep."

Ronica smiled at that. "I know the feeling. It's your mind. It won't stop."

"I'm worried about Charlie."

Ronica sat on the edge of the bed. "What in particular?"

"I wanted him to be a doctor. He has the ability; he just needs to recognize it. He'll never do that if I'm gone."

"You and Josiah have raised Charlie to know what he wants. Whatever happens, he will be okay. And you know Josiah will always be there for him."

Her eyes opened, wandering slowly over Ronica's face. "You love him."

"Charlie?" Ronica did love the boy. He was kind, considerate, and respectful—like his father.

"My husband."

Ronica's heart felt squeezed as if from an invisible hand. There was no hiding it. "Yes. Josiah is my best friend, and he was Fletcher's too."

Olivia's lips twisted. "And if Josiah weren't married? Then what?"

Weariness overcame Ronica in a rush. "He *is* still married, thanks to you. So I guess we'll never know."

"Oh, you'll be there to comfort him when I'm gone." The bitterness in her voice was thick enough to feel like a slap. "I have no doubt."

Anger reared its ugly head, escaping her mouth before Ronica could stop it. "Don't try to play the victim here, Olivia. I know you. You broke his heart. And I suspect you plan to do it again. But for the record, he's been loyal to you, even if you haven't been to him."

"Get out!" Olivia snapped, although the words were too breathy to have the desired effect.

"Sorry." Ronica smiled wryly. "You're stuck with me. You're stuck with all of us. The town of Forgotten doesn't desert its own."

Olivia's nostrils flared. "You think I deserve this."

Ronica considered that as the anger seeped from her. "No more than my husband deserved to lose his mind. You haven't made a lot of friends, but no one wants you to die."

Olivia's body relaxed, and for a time they sat in silence. Then Olivia whispered, "I don't want to die, either. I thought . . . I thought with Josiah's goodness on my side that maybe things would change for me . . . that maybe . . ."

She closed her eyes and didn't speak again until Natalie brought her the smoothie. "Thank you," Olivia said, allowing them to help her sit up enough to put the straw in her mouth.

"There's more in the fridge." Natalie jerked a thumb over her shoulder in the direction of the kitchen. "It won't be as good the second time, but blended with a little ice, it'll be good enough. I'm taking off now for my meeting." She looked between them, noting their sober expressions. "Did I miss something?"

"No." Ronica shook her head. "Have fun."

"I will. I'm looking forward to meeting these people." She paused before adding, "I hope they're not all weirdos."

Ronica laughed with her, then scooted closer to help Olivia with the smoothie.

Olivia waved her away. "I can do it."

She sipped while Ronica signed into her streaming platform and began searching for something to watch.

"Oh, no," Olivia muttered with a panicked breath. "Take this." She shoved the smoothie at Ronica and reached for something in her large handbag next to her on the bed.

A bowl.

She retched inside it, throwing up smoothie. She continued retching long after anything came out. When the convulsions stopped, Ronica asked quietly, "Is there anything I can do?"

"No." Olivia dabbed at her mouth with a disposable wipe from the handbag. "I will probably keep the rest down now. Maybe."

She did, sipping slowly and pausing at length between swallows. "Is there a mirror here you can bring me?" she asked at one pause. "The one in my purse isn't very big."

"I haven't seen any except in the bathroom," Ronica said. "But you look beautiful as always. You don't need to worry about that." It was true—except now her beauty had a layer of fragility that hadn't existed before.

"Thank you." Olivia seemed content with her words. She took two more sips before reaching for the remote and starting a show. After a few moments, she said, "I wasn't a good wife."

Ronica shifted her eyes from the television to her. "No, you weren't."

Olivia sighed. "I like that you don't lie to me. You might be the only person who never does. Even Josiah."

"He's not a liar."

Her lips twitched. "No. He just changes the subject."

Ronica was about to say that wasn't true, but maybe it was with Olivia, who had hurt him so deeply. She wanted to ask what Olivia's intentions were, but Josiah had made his choice, and that meant it was none of her business.

With the smoothie finally finished and Olivia dozing quietly,

Ronica had little recollection of the show Olivia had chosen for them to watch. Leaving the door open in case Olivia called out, Ronica went to the kitchen to wash the glass and then scrubbed the sick bowl in the bathroom, placing it next to Olivia again on one of the towels. A despair she hadn't felt since Fletcher's diagnosis built inside her. This would be Josiah's life for however long it took, and she would be by his side because no one should have to face this alone, not him and not even Olivia.

Once back in the living room, she texted Josiah. *Everything's okay here, but in case Olivia didn't text you, I think the treatment didn't work as planned. They're doing another in the morning, so I'll get her home later than we thought. Not by much. But I need to talk to you, so give me a call when you can. It's about Charlie.*

The phone rang almost immediately, as she suspected it would. City meetings were almost always in the morning, and this close to the end of the day when everyone was getting ready to leave, he'd be able to step aside momentarily for information about Charlie. And not just because of Charlie, she knew, but because she'd asked. It was better this way over the phone, because if he were here right now, she didn't know if she could stop herself from weeping in his arms, and that might not be wise, given the feelings she had for him and him for her.

She closed her eyes briefly to center herself before answering. "Hey," she greeted. "What's up?"

"Just going over the budget. With the donation last fall from the Coxes, I think we'll be able to afford the repairs on the road to Panna Creek. It won't be in time for the Spring Planting Dance because we'll need those proceeds too, but if it's as big a success as you made it last year, we'll be able to do it."

The familiar timbre of his voice comforted her, and she was relieved at the casual conversation—as if death wasn't haunting both of them, or as if they weren't yearning for more inside their hearts.

"I'll make sure it's the best year ever," she promised. "Too bad we can't get it finished before the spring rain. People will be stranded as usual."

"Unless we can come up with a new large town event or fundraiser, that won't happen. Last I checked, Valentine's and St. Patrick's Day party proceeds only cover the actual celebrations. But the way I figure it, the rains will be fresh in people's minds by the Spring Planting Dance, and they'll participate more, which will give us the funds we need."

She laughed. "Good point."

He let a few polite seconds pass before asking, "So what's this about Charlie?"

"I don't want to break his confidence, so I'm not telling you right out, but you need to stop and think about how this is affecting him."

"He's worried about Olivia, naturally."

"His concern isn't about Olivia. Charlie knows what's up with her. It's you, Josiah. I know it's tempting because of what I've gone through with Fletcher, but you can't stop living. You can't stop feeling joy and love and all the rest of the good things. Charlie needs you to be you."

A whoosh of breath told her he'd understood. "I've been so wrapped up in—"

"I know," she interrupted. "It's him you need to tell. Make him understand. You're good at that. Spend a lot of alone time with him. You've always put him first, and he needs you to do that now."

"Okay, and thanks."

He was silent so for long she thought he might have hung up, but then he spoke again, his beautiful voice low. "How are you doing?"

"I'm okay. Not fine yet, but I will be. And so will you."

"I'll take your word for it." He sounded lost.

She steeled herself against feeling too much for him. "I'm hanging up now. I got up way too early today, so I'm going to take a little nap until Olivia wakes."

"I can never repay you for this."

"I'm not doing this just for you," she said, which was mostly the truth. She also wanted to help Olivia for Charlie and Keisha, and even for Fletcher, who in her mind was connected to Olivia's family because Josiah had helped her so much with him.

"Goodbye," she said. Silently, she added, I love you.

"Goodbye."

As she set her phone on the coffee table, a cry came from the bedroom. Ronica popped up from the sofa. "I'm coming," she called.

CHAPTER 12

Natalie McColl felt awkward walking into the room at the local library where the estranged parents of adult children planned to meet. Someone had set out a table of refreshments, and a woman there urged people to grab a plate before sitting in chairs that formed a circle. There were only eight people there, with Natalie and her ride, a woman named Lois, making ten so far. Lois, a confident, dark-haired woman in business attire, was the group member who had first connected with her in the online group after learning she lived so close to Lincoln. She didn't look like an abandoned mother. She didn't seem to have the stamp *rejected* that Natalie felt on her own forehead.

The most awkward thing in attending this meeting was the fact that everyone in this room knew her own child had cut her off and walked away. They might not know that Joni had called her abusive and blamed her for every problem in her life, but they knew Natalie had been abandoned. She felt like a twisted deviant trying to fool the world into thinking she was normal.

At the same time, it was comforting to know that all these

people also had children who had cut them off, often without an explanation, and it was this knowledge that made her brave enough to come.

I am normal, I am good, I am kind, I am enough. It was a litany she told herself so she could put one foot in front of the other instead of staying in bed waiting to die.

"Hungry?" Lois paused near the food table.

Natalie's stomach churned too much to want snacks, though she'd barely eaten that day. "I don't think I can eat."

Lois smiled at her with compassion. "It gets easier. Why don't you go sit down, and I'll grab us something."

Natalie took the first chair on the right side, where her back wouldn't be toward the door. She wanted to make sure she could see anyone else who entered. During the time at the cancer center, she'd begun having second thoughts about attending tonight, wondering how healthy the group might actually be. A few of the parents seemed to be as entitled as they claimed their children were. Some posted screenshots of texts they sent to their children that curdled her blood because she'd never speak to someone she despised like that, much less a child she loved with all her heart.

As the wife of the police chief of Forgotten, she'd learned to be a peacemaker in town, and some words were simply fighting words. If a person shouldn't say them to a stranger, why would they say them to an adult child? And yet those parents' children would at least text back, usually cursing and wishing their parents dead, demanding money, or listing all their faults, but at least they texted. For months now, her Joni simply hadn't answered. As if Natalie were so unimportant that she really didn't care if she lost her forever. The only reason Natalie knew Joni wasn't dead and lying in a gutter somewhere was that Natalie was still paying her phone bill, and she could see it was in use, even if she couldn't see any other information. It gave her some small relief—unless she thought too deeply about who might actually be using the phone.

Pulling her mind away from the depressing thoughts, she went back to studying the other parents. So far, they looked normal, primarily women from different walks of life and from every race and color. Most had dressed up in nice pants or dresses, but one wore jeans. There was only one man, barrel-chested with a short blond beard, who was making his way toward the circle of chairs, balancing a full plate on his flannel-covered arm and carrying a cup in his other hand.

He set his drink down as he sat beside her. "Hi, I'm Gary." He held out his big hand, engulfing hers as she shook it. He didn't look like a father whose child hated him. He looked easy-going and fun, like someone who'd love bouncing a grandchild on his lap and wouldn't care if the child smeared him all over with peanut butter.

"Natalie." She gave him a polite smile.

"Nice to meet you." He took a bite of cheese and crackers from his plate. "This meeting is a cool idea."

"Yeah. I think so too." Maybe. She wasn't really sure. She was still embarrassed and deeply ashamed that she was the kind of person who'd been rejected by her child.

"Son or daughter?" Gary asked after a few minutes.

She blinked in puzzlement before she understood that he was asking about her estrangement. Why did she feel so slow and clumsy? "Daughter," she said, the ever-present knot of shame and remorse building in her chest.

He gave her a sympathetic smile. "Me too. I'm sorry." He didn't say anything more, and the pressure inside her eased.

"I'm sorry too," she managed.

"Thanks." He took another bite and chewed.

Others were joining the circle now, some smiling, a few seeming dazed and avoiding eye contact. Some chatted as they found places to sit. Lois came toward Natalie with two plates, smiling as she handed her one and sat on her other side.

"Thanks," Natalie muttered.

Almost everyone was seated when an older couple came through the door, moving slowly. The woman's eyes were swollen, her face pallid and vacant as if she'd come from bed after a long illness. The man was practically supporting her, his narrow face tight and angry. They didn't head for the food table but toward two empty seats, the man pulling his chair closer to his wife's before sitting.

"For me, it's been six years," Gary said, drawing Natalie's attention back to him. "Happened when I got divorced. I don't really know how exactly, but one day about six months after the divorce when she was still seventeen, she refused to come over for my visitation days, and the more I fought for her, the more she pushed me away. By the time she was nineteen and in college, she was saying I was an abusive father who never did anything for her. All she wanted was for me to fork over all kinds of cash, but otherwise I was ordered to stay out of her life."

The money part sounded familiar to Natalie. Joni always needed money—or at least that was what usually brought her back after another disappearance. That and a place to stay.

"Sounds awful." She poked the crackers on her plate. "I'm sorry. You still don't see her?"

He shook his head. "At first it was like a raw wound that occupied every moment of my day, and for a while, I didn't think I was going to make it. But after a few years, I finally made the choice to live. For real. Not like a zombie."

Murmurs of approval scattered through the room, and Natalie looked around to see Gary had everyone's attention now.

"How did you do that?" Lois asked him. "Make that choice, I mean? For me, it was when I spent a week in a mental hospital, and the therapist helped me understand my worth and that my husband and sister needed me. Being involved with my sister's kids and befriending a neighbor couple with a new baby saved me."

Natalie stared at her, surprised. She and Lois had talked a lot online, and she knew about Lois's thirty-something daughter who cut her off after a disagreement, taking away the granddaughter who had lived with Lois for three of her five years, but she hadn't expected a mental hospital stay from a woman who looked as if she had everything together.

"I don't know exactly how I made the choice." Gary frowned as he appeared to consider. "But I remember when it happened. One day my daughter was screaming at me over the phone for asking to come to her graduation—after all, I'd paid for her college— and then suddenly I realized it didn't matter how much I groveled or tried to make amends for mistakes I'd made when she was a child. Her mother had poisoned her against me. I couldn't bear another deranged screaming fit from someone who so obviously hated me, so I decided that I either needed to pull the trigger and be done with life, or I had to walk away and protect myself. Fortunately, I had parents who needed me, and a supportive cousin, so I walked away." His smile came readily enough, and Natalie couldn't detect any sadness in his eyes. "That was a year ago. It's a lot easier now that I'm dating someone whose adult children really like me. I'm probably going to ask her to marry me." He gave Natalie a grin. "She doesn't even mind the flannel shirts my ex-wife claims ruined our marriage." Light laughter met this comment.

"Anyway," Gary continued, "that's really why I wanted to come tonight—to meet those of you whose stories have inspired me and to tell all of you that there's a light on the other side. I still hope someday my daughter will step away from her mother a bit and see me as a person, but if she never does, I will still be the kind of person who can love and be there for others. She doesn't get to define the rest of my life."

More nods and agreement, but then the older lady who had walked in with her husband said, "What if I don't want a life on the other side?" She hiccupped a tiny sob before continuing. "All I ever wanted was to have a family, and she's our only child.

My daughter and I were so close, and now she won't even let me see my three grandchildren."

As the woman spoke, Natalie realized the woman wasn't as old as she'd first thought. Probably in her early fifties, though the pinched grief on her face made her look at least a decade older.

"Her husband hates me," the woman continued, tears coming to her puffy eyes. "He says I'm a bad influence."

"For letting the kids go into our backyard in pajamas!" her husband spat. "Melinda, it was ridiculous six months ago, and it's still ridiculous now!"

"I should have changed them first. I was going to wash the clothes after, though. I didn't know it would cause this rift."

The man's jaw tightened. "It's pajamas," he hissed through gritted teeth. "Our generation slept outside in our pajamas in tree houses, and we didn't die or contract some dire illness. That son-in-law of ours looks for ways to punish and criticize. First, it's making them say please for every little thing, as if they have to beg for a stupid sandwich, and then freaking out at us for using the wrong kind of toothpaste." His gaze fell on Natalie. "Apparently, I was supposed to drive thirty minutes at nine at night to find the right kind because they forgot to put it in the overnight bag. Does that make sense?"

Natalie shook her head, wondering if she should respond verbally, but the man's gaze swept onward through the group. "Then I left the steaks on the grill too long at our daughter's birthday dinner, and somehow that meant I disrespected him. He's a narcissistic bully, and our daughter doesn't have the spine to stand up to him."

"Wow, that's awful." Lois's eyebrow hiked up on her forehead, and Natalie nodded in agreement.

"I have a similar thing happening with my son," said a woman with kinky black hair and dark skin. "If you don't appease the gate-keeper, you get nothing. My daughter-in-law became offended at some offhanded comment I made about refined foods, and now she won't let me see my son or grandson no matter how many apologies I make or how many boatloads of eggshells I tiptoe across. Her family gets all the holidays and birthdays. We get nothing. I'm Cherry, by the way, and I thank God every day that I have a daughter and two other grandchildren. They are my salvation."

This caused a sniff from Melinda. "I should have had other children." She cast a dark look at her husband, but instead of reacting in anger at her obvious accusation, he took her hand and nodded. It was probably an old conversation, and Natalie realized that beneath his bluster, he was hurting as much as his wife.

"My daughter kicked me out because I didn't want to get rid of my cat," said a plain woman in a droopy gray sweater. "Just because my cat messed on her carpet, and I didn't clean it and all the dishes before she got home from work, she got mad and made me leave." She glared at all of them. "Can you believe that? Tossing your own mother out on the street! And I'm on social security. I told her kids they'd better be careful, or she'll throw them out too. She's so mean to them. Never lets them do anything fun, and I'm not afraid to say that right to their faces. The names she called me." Rolling her eyes, she proceeded to state very colorfully everything her daughter had said and her own vicious replies.

For a moment, no one spoke. Often it was the parents demanding accountability—rent, phone payments, getting a job, stopping the drugs, and being respectful that set the twenty-something adult child on the road to estrangement. Some kids had to learn everything the hard way. But this story seemed to be the opposite.

A thin blond woman, who Natalie recognized as Claire Rogers, the moderator of the online group, spoke first. "Edith, it's really sad that you and your daughter are estranged. I know it hurts. When we last talked online, you said you were trying to get into some housing. Did you do that? Yes? Good. Do you feel you can support yourself now? That's a good first step."

Melinda's husband rolled his eyes. "I don't get it." He pointed at

Edith. "You want your daughter to support you? You're the mother. I'm not saying you should support her, but expecting her to pay your bills seems a bit out there."

"I took care of her for twenty years all by myself!" Edith shot back. "It's not like I'm that much of a burden. I paid for my food and part of the rent and watched the kids. That actually helped her too, you know."

"Yeah, but if you're undermining her authority with your grandkids, that's a trainwreck waiting to happen," Cherry said, her voice soft. "I don't perfectly approve of everything my non-estranged daughter and her husband do with their kids, but I keep my mouth absolutely shut. My opinions really aren't any more important than theirs, and they're not my kids. I'm just there to be Grandma. I'd never dream of saying anything bad about their parents in front of them—or really at all, come to think of it."

"I'm only helping them!" Edith nearly shouted, red flushing her narrow face.

"Okay, everyone," Claire interjected, giving her hands a sharp clap. "Let's dial it back a bit. Remember that we are all at different stages in our estrangement. We aren't here to judge but to support." Edith nodded vigorously, her round eyes flashing in triumph.

Natalie decided Edith was either showing a tough outer shell or she hadn't begun to look inside herself to see what she should be working on to repair her relationship. Either way, her pain was still real.

When no one else spoke, Claire began talking. "Most of you know my story. I was busy working when my two daughters were growing up, and they blamed me for the divorce, which is true because I couldn't take his emotional abuse anymore. Their father gave me full custody in exchange for almost no child support, but now that they're married, they're in tight with him and his new wife. He has a lot of money and basically bribes them. I would get one or two texts a year, and I was permitted to send presents to the grandchildren and to see them twice a year online, but that's as far as it went. He made them choose, and they chose him because of what he could buy for them. It was that way for seven years, and then I cut things off." A steely note entered her voice. "I couldn't live that half life anymore. Like many of you, I'm remarried, and my husband's children have become my family. He actually wasn't a great father while they were growing up, but he's come a long way, and we all have a great relationship. It's good to have holidays again with people who love and respect me."

"But it still hurts." This from Melinda.

Claire sighed. "Only if I let myself dwell on it. I think as mothers—and fathers, too—we will always wish that our children were in our lives, but we absolutely can't stop living because our children continue to have issues and refuse to take any responsibility for their actions and choices."

"But my son remembers things that never happened," put in a woman with a red braid. She was younger than the others and had the look of one who had once been strikingly beautiful but was now beaten and worn. "I was only seventeen when I had him, but I did everything I could to give him a good life. He's twenty now and says he's hated me since he was six, and that cutting me out of his life is the only way he can be happy. He sends me the most vile texts if I try to reach out, and I have no idea why he's mad at me. Where does he get this?"

"From crappy therapists, TikTok, and other social media outlets." Gary rolled his eyes. "It's a badge of courage for this throwaway generation to cut off their parents and an act of cowardice not to do so. They're urged to cut off anyone who annoys them, without even opening a dialogue for the most part. Then they are praised and supported for doing so. They throw around psychological terms, diagnosing everyone except themselves. Their favorite is that we are narcissistic, which is rarely the case. And I know because my ex-wife actually has that diagnosis. Anyway, our children have been taught by the world to care only about themselves. They don't care about the generational damage estrangement causes."

"Generational?" asked Melinda. "You mean my grandkids might later estrange themselves from their parents? That would kill my daughter. She dotes on them. It'd kill her like it's killing me."

"Well, it's what they're being taught," Lois said with a shrug "To run instead of working it out. So possibly."

"Yes, that too, but I was thinking more along the lines of the lack of support from grandparents," Gary said. "Even though mine were old-fashioned, according to my parents, I loved visiting my grandparents because they'd actually play with me and weren't busy. They put me first. And as a teenager and young adult, they were very instrumental in helping me figure out schooling and my career. My grandchildren will never know that love from me."

Natalie couldn't help the tears that escaped her eyes at his words. Joni's children would also not have her love. A few of the others were nodding and crying too, and Natalie realized what horrible abuse these strangers were enduring from those they loved so very much.

"I was estranged from my mom," Edith said into the silence. "But my mom was extremely abusive. She used to have her boyfriend beat me with a belt if I ever did anything wrong, and I can't tell you how many days I ate food out of the neighbor's garbage because she couldn't be bothered."

Everyone was shocked at the admission, and Natalie was devastated for her. "That's terrible." Claire's eyebrows furrowed. "I know I speak for all of us in saying that."

"I vowed my daughter would never have to do that, and she didn't." Edith looked down her fingers as if unable to bear their pity.

A few heartbeats of silence passed, and then the red-haired lady asked, "Will they ever see what they're doing? Will they ever come back? I miss my son so much."

A few shrugged, and one or two nodded hopefully.

"We can only hope they do," Claire said with a sigh, "and that it's not too late. The damage these children are doing to an entire generation of parents who did their best really is too awful for words. But it's also true that many parents still don't see their own part in the estrangement—not saying any of you, of course, but so many others I've worked with don't understand what the issue is. Sadly, without the dialogue that most of the estranged children refuse to have, it's impossible to figure out."

"Or the cryptic talk," the red-haired woman added. "Saying things but not explaining in a way we can understand."

"Right." Claire waved a finger at her in agreement.

Melinda let out a sob and curled into her husband's arm. "For us, I think it's not really our daughter's fault." He patted her on the back, his face softening. "But I don't know if she'll find the courage to do anything except what her husband makes her do."

Over the next ninety minutes, more stories emerged. A girl who suddenly distanced herself at twenty and asked for space. A boy strung out on drugs, who robbed his family home before disappearing. A thirty-year-old who accepted a thirty-thousand dollar down payment for a home before cutting his parents off, his teenage children no longer allowed to talk to their grandmother, whose heart was shattered. On and on the stories continued, many of the situations complicated by well-meaning or purposefully hurtful relatives, some stepping in to take the place of parents until they too stepped the wrong way and were abandoned. Most of the parents admitted some fault in the estrangement and talked of their confusion at why their children wouldn't simply sit down to work things out.

"They treat strangers better than family." Lois shook her head and frowned. "My daughter is also on social media saying how difficult motherhood is and for her friends not to judge themselves so harshly, but I am not allowed to make any mistakes."

"They're spoiled rotten brats," muttered Melinda's husband.

"I just can't believe it," Melinda murmured. "It feels like she has a sledgehammer and keeps hitting me over and over." Nods of agreement came from almost everyone in attendance.

"Like heart surgery without anesthesia," said another mother.

"Like being thrown down a garbage disposal," Gary said.

Lois nodded. "Or a paper in a shredder."

"It's like they erased me." Claire moved her hand as if wiping something away. "Like I was just a surrogate mother for my ex and his new wife."

Natalie's eyes filled with tears that rolled down her cheeks in rivulets. The pain in the room felt like a smothering blanket that threatened to choke the life from her. Yet at the same time, she was incredibly grateful because these people really understood the yearning, shame, heartache, and intoxicating pain that had become her life. They weren't like anyone else she'd tried to talk to. These broken parents lived her life daily. Constantly. Even Edith, who was likely more responsible for her estrangement than her daughter, understood the horrendous pain.

"What about you?" Edith asked, looking at Natalie, who'd kept her silence. "What's your story?"

Natalie's eyes dropped to the plate in her lap, surprised to see she had eaten whatever Lois had put on it. She vaguely remembered a slice of cheese and a piece of something that might have been banana bread.

"You don't have to tell us," Gary assured her quickly. "It's hard, especially at first."

"It's not really the first time," Natalie said. "My daughter is twenty-five, and this is the third time she's disappeared from my life. But it's the first time she told me not to contact her. It's been eight months now, and I'm just . . . I'm so worried. She looked like a skeleton the last time I saw her."

"Does she have a mental illness?" asked a woman whose daughter had been diagnosed with borderline personality disorder.

Natalie shrugged. "I don't know. She's always been . . . well, she's never been able to tell the truth. Not ever. And with my husband being the police chief, you can imagine there was some conflict there, but she never seemed to care what punishment we gave her. She used to sneak out at night, and I know she used to break into our liquor cabinet. At one point, I stopped buying alcohol altogether, but she always knew how to get what she wanted. She is likely an alcoholic. I worry that . . ." That she'd die alone. But those words wouldn't leave her mouth.

"It's not your fault." Lois reached over to rest a hand on her arm. "Nothing you did or didn't do could change this. You have to give yourself grace. You are a good person, and you love your daughter. Anyone can tell that."

"I would do anything for her," Natalie admitted. "I just don't know what more I can do. If I knew I had done something wrong, I would ask for forgiveness. In fact, I already asked forgiveness for anything I could think of."

"That's a mistake," Gary said with a snort. "It only gives them more weapons to use against you because you definitely remember their childhood better than they do. I mean, I'm all for writing an amends letter like the good reconciliation therapists say to do, but you should only apologize for whatever your kid says you did, or what you know you did—if you have any clue. Don't give her more reasons to hate you than she already has. Like my daughter didn't need to know that sometimes after work, I'd stop to buy her a donut as a treat, and then I'd get stuck in traffic and eat it myself, and not even tell her I bought it. When I confessed that to her in the beginning of the estrangement, it made her think I was even more selfish than I really am."

Claire nodded. "Actually, he's right. We need to look inside ourselves and try to understand what they're saying we did wrong and why they feel that way. We should apologize for mistakes and make our relationship a safe place for them. And we need to meet them where they are currently, because in the beginning, they're simply not capable of seeing any of their own fault in the situation. However, this doesn't mean we have to accept blame for things we didn't do, or for all their poor choices and where they ended up because of them." She smiled and dipped her head at Gary. "Or for donuts they didn't expect to get."

"Should I write an amends letter then?" Natalie had been researching them, but they seemed to be exactly what she'd already sent by text and email, except that in them she admitted to how much the estrangement hurt her—and apparently that kind of guilt pushed many estranged kids further away.

"If you've already tried, then let a little more time go by," Claire advised. "Six months or another year. You have to respect her wishes. And in the meantime, you work on you. Work on finding joy."

"I think amends letters are crap," said Edith with a grimace. "They basically want you to plead guilty for every mistake you made in your life. These kids want perfect parents. Even if they treat you like garbage ninety percent of the time."

Claire shook her head and said quickly, "I have to disagree. I think many adult children just need to know they are heard, and yes, they might not be able to listen to anything that might include any hint of guilt for themselves because they are too hurt. But maybe later as the relationship redevelops, they'll see that they hurt their parents too."

"Do you have other kids?" Gary asked Natalie. "Grandkids?"

Natalie nodded. "Another daughter. No grandkids yet. And I know having another daughter who cares makes me one of the lucky ones, but somehow that doesn't seem to fill the hole in my heart, even though my younger daughter has put me through the worst pain I have ever experienced. Some days, I just want it to end." She hesitated and added, "I pray never to wake up."

"We've all been there." Claire's face was sympathetic. "And facing that pain is the right place to start. But ultimately, you deserve more. We all do. We all have those really bad days where we don't get out of bed because we can't stop crying, but there are things we can do to pull ourselves out of the despair. Maybe we can talk about the tools we can use to make sure we keep healing ourselves. Therapy can help, if you haven't tried that, but doing things you love is also very good. Keeping busy, you know."

"Fake it till you make it," Gary quipped.

"For me, connecting with others helped the most," Lois said. "And getting a dog."

"It was finding new hobbies I really love that changed my focus," Cherry said. "Well, the therapy too, and realizing that I can keep my relationship with my other child healthy by respecting her boundaries and maintaining my own."

Other self-help suggestions Natalie wrote down on her phone included volunteering at a school, going on trips with friends, serving in a church or the community, and reaching out to extended family. Basically, it meant focusing on her own life instead of worrying about something she was powerless to fix.

"The worst might happen," Gary observed, "and she might never come back, but it might not, and even if the worst does happen, you will go on because you have no choice." He grimaced. "Well, there is that other choice, but that's not really any choice. That's giving up. We deserve peace, but in the end, we're the only ones who can claim it."

Natalie felt guilty even thinking about feeling joy while things were so awful with Joni. But really, what choice did she have? Her husband needed her, her older daughter needed her, and her friends needed her. She needed to choose life.

As she and Lois walked out to the car after the meeting, Lois said, "I know it all seems impossible right now, but slowly the part of you that is dying will reverse and come back to life. You just have to be diligent."

"Actually, I think I feel a lot better." Natalie gave her a smile. "Somehow it helps to see that some of those people have it much worse than I do. And it's comforting to know they understand. I've talked to a few friends, but I don't know how much they get, you know?"

"Oh, do I. It's hard sometimes to find people who understand what you're going through. For the longest time, I could barely talk to anyone because I was so ashamed and heartbroken. It gets really old to keep bleeding your pain all over where your friends can see. Most simply do not have the frame of reference to begin to understand."

"Right. That's exactly what it feels like. Bleeding constantly. But after tonight and this week in the group, I think I need to change my whole focus." She gave a wry chuckle. "It might take a while."

"At least a year or two," Lois agreed as she beeped her car open. "But it would be a lot longer if you didn't start the journey, right? You really do deserve peace. You must believe that even if you believe nothing else."

"I'll try. I just wish I knew why she doesn't want me." Natalie hesitated with her hand on the passenger door.

Lois shook her head. "We may never know. And you know what? I think I'm at the point many other parents have reached where maybe dwelling on the why isn't the best use of time. Our daughters may never want to talk about it, even if we reconcile, and we will have to live with that."

Natalie's heart seemed to lighten a bit with the idea as she fastened her safety belt. Maybe Lois was right. Maybe the only important thing was if she could help and love her daughter.

She waited until Lois started the car to ask the other question that had been burning inside her. "Have you seen any of these estrangements end in reconciliation?"

"Oh, yes. A lot of them. Usually within a few years." She sighed. "After that, it's far more difficult."

"And is it the same between the mothers and kids? Joni and I were very close once. We even started a business together. But since she's disappeared before, I admit I haven't felt the same because it's always there in my mind, the knowing that she could walk away. She doesn't love me the same way I love her or care about my feelings. She's willing to hurt me, and that's a horrible thing to know about your kid."

Lois thought for a minute. "I think it depends on the reason for the estrangement. If it's more about the child's life journey and finding their way, then I've had women tell me that the relationship feels normal and complete to them. But the moms have also learned better communication and boundaries, so maybe that's part of it. But for mothers whose children are mentally ill, have addiction problems, or whose children simply don't value them . . . so mothers like you and me, because I think my daughter struggles with some mental issues . . ." She glanced over at Natalie as she came to a stop at a traffic light. "For us, I think we'll always need to protect ourselves."

She held out her right hand, palm up. "I got this to remind me to always remember to protect my heart. I don't actually like tattoos, but I needed something to constantly remind me that I deserve more."

"Tattoo?" Natalie peered closer and finally spied a tiny heart at the base of her ring finger. It was unobtrusive but definitely something Lois would be able to see when she needed a shot of protection. "Oh, it's nice."

"I have to touch it up way too often because of the location, but maybe one day I won't need it anymore, and I'll let it go." Lois moved the car forward as the light changed. "Some members of our group get really big ones with something to remind them to focus on the positive. But I think it would bring too many questions, and those are painful. I wanted something only for me. I still hope I can repair the relationship one day, but I understand I can never let myself trust her as much as I did before. I cannot allow myself to ever think I deserve death because my daughter won't talk to me or forgive me for a mistake. Ultimately, I need to do my part, and to be honest, I'm still working on that, but if she doesn't work to fix it too, then that says more about her than it does about me."

Natalie nodded. "I don't know if Joni will ever get better. Or if she'll want to work on anything."

"I'm sorry."

"Thanks. And before now, only my husband and a friend knew about the alcohol. I never wanted people to see her in a negative light, you know?"

"Makes sense. I don't share my story with anyone at all anymore, not even family. Only to the group, where we are all in a sort of therapy."

"Right. Though frankly, with parents like Edith, . . . well, I can kind of see why their kids might want to distance themselves." Natalie felt judgmental even as she said it because she didn't really know the details or how much bravado Edith faked to hide her pain.

"Yeah," Lois agreed. "But it doesn't explain their children's utter cruelty or how they treat strangers better than their own parents. Anyway, most of the parents, even those who had a part in the estrangement, remedy their behavior and try really hard. But it's like their children are just . . . gone upstairs. No reasoning or compassion. Like my daughter." Lois flashed her a sad smile before looking at the road again.

"It's hard to accept that I might never talk to my baby again. But maybe I should close the door like Claire did. It would almost hurt less." As Natalie spoke, she could feel a hint of freedom hovering just out of reach. Freedom from pain and bondage and guilt.

"Alcoholism is a disease," Lois said. "And that means you will need to be there to pick up the pieces when they fall. That's what mothers do, even abandoned mothers like us."

"I guess you're right. Whatever happens, thanks for inviting me and picking me up. It's been enlightening."

Fifteen minutes later when Natalie walked into the apartment, she found Ronica sitting on the couch, snacking from a bowl of popcorn and watching something on the large television so softly that it would be a miracle if she could follow the plot.

"Olivia?" Natalie asked.

"Sleeping," Ronica whispered, darting a glance toward Olivia's open door. "Finally. But only after taking something to help her sleep. She drank all the smoothie you gave her and the rest in the fridge. I also gave her peanut butter on bread and sticks of cheese that she brought with her. I could tell she didn't want to eat any of it, but she insisted on trying. Do you have enough for another smoothie in the morning?"

"I do. Yes."

Ronica's eyes narrowed. "What about you? Are you okay? How did it go?"

Natalie sat down next to her friend. "Truthfully, it was heart-breaking. I don't think a single parent there deserved what's happening except maybe one woman, and with her I think it's more for lack of education. I'm not saying they haven't all made mistakes. Everyone admitted to some fault—well, except the missing adult children, of course." Natalie sighed and fell silent.

Ronica leaned back. "Don't stop. I'm all ears if you want to share."

"Actually, I'm all talked out." All bled out, she meant, but Ronica didn't need to picture that analogy. "But thank you for offering."

"Popcorn?"

Natalie leaned over for a handful. "I'm suddenly starving—and utterly exhausted. I'm going to make myself something and crash out here on the sofa so I can keep an ear out for Olivia. Why don't you go upstairs and be with Laina and the others? You've been here alone long enough."

Ronica placed the popcorn on the coffee table. "I believe I will. But text me if you need me. Olivia has her phone if she needs to text either of us, so don't be too concerned. She was pretty out the last time I checked, so we can probably shut the door now."

Natalie had barely sat down in front of the flickering television when a text came in from her husband, Caleb.

You having a good time, sweetheart?

Yeah, it's been good.

He'd been supportive about the meeting, even if he hadn't wanted to join in.

Now a good time to talk? he asked.

Sure. As long as it wasn't about Joni, she'd love to talk to him. Caleb really was her world right now, and she needed to concentrate on their life together.

The phone buzzed, and she answered quietly. "Hi."

"Hi." He paused before rushing on. "Look, honey, I'm sorry to blurt it out this way, but I have news about Joni."

Her heart leapt with what might be a little portion of joy, which momentarily confused her. How could there be any hope left?

"What is it? Did she text you?" Natalie thought it highly unlikely their daughter would text him first.

"No. The police in Panna Creek contacted me. The ambulance picked her up, and the hospital reached out to them to find next of kin. They had her driver's license."

Panic blotted out the joy. "Is she all right?"

"I called the hospital, and they said she's heavily sedated at the moment. And stable. So that's good, I think."

Natalie's mind raced. "I can rent a car and be there in a few hours." She started to say goodbye.

"Honey, wait." His voice compelled her to listen. "They said she won't wake up until morning at the earliest. And they won't know much before the tests come back anyway—and that's also in the morning. So here's what I think we should do. I'll go sit with her now, and maybe Ronica can drop you off on your way back to town. I'd feel a lot better if you didn't drive alone. You know how your night vision is."

Everything inside Natalie screamed in protest. She needed to get to her baby!

"Please, honey," he pressed.

She sighed. Her logical side knew her husband was right because she wasn't comfortable driving at night, and with this news about her daughter . . . well, she wasn't entirely sure she would be able to stop crying long enough to see where she was going.

"I'll keep you informed," he added. "And Doc Sayer promised to come in the morning and take a look at her as well."

"Okay," she agreed reluctantly. "But you have to promise to let me know what's going on. I want to know the second she's awake."

"I promise. Don't worry. I will stay with her all night."

Natalie's appetite deserted her once again, but this time because of hope—the four-letter word that could be more painful than any other word in the dictionary.

Would this be a new beginning for them, or was it the end?

CHAPTER 13

Ronica drove a little faster than she ordinarily did after they left Lincoln. Olivia's visit early that morning to the cancer center had gone much quicker than the day before, presumably because they'd worked her in before their regularly scheduled appointments, and with it being a weekend, there weren't as many of those to begin with.

Afterward, Olivia had been terribly nauseated, but she hadn't complained or spoken since they put her in the Lexus and started for home. She was now dozing, clutching her sick bowl like a lifeline. She'd acted horribly embarrassed at being this frail in front of them, and Ronica wondered what it might mean for Josiah if she refused their help in the future.

Riding in the back seat, Natalie was a nervous wreck, her eyes haunted and rimmed in the red of someone who had cried more than she had slept. She kept texting her husband, but he only told her that their daughter was still unconscious and that he was waiting for the doctor to come in to talk to him.

"He's not telling me everything," Natalie muttered. "I can tell."

Ronica thought so too, but she wanted to ease her friend's anxiety. "We'll be there soon. Don't worry."

"He promised to tell me." Natalie's voice rose a bit. "He doesn't lie."

Ronica thought he might leave a little out to protect her, but she couldn't say as much.

"I could text Xander," Keisha spoke up suddenly from where she sat next to Natalie. "He's on rotation today, and he might be able to find out something." She'd come with them instead of Laina because she was needed to drive Olivia the rest of the way home after dropping Natalie and Ronica off at the hospital in Panna Creek.

Natalie looked at her eagerly. "Please. He can give me the information, right? Since I'm her next of kin."

"I think so. Unless she's married."

Natalie sucked in a breath. "I really don't know."

"Well, since she's unconscious, it might not matter unless a husband is there hanging around."

"Caleb said a male friend called the ambulance, but that he's not there now. We don't know how close of a friend."

Keisha was silent as she texted. "Okay, there we have it. I don't know how long it will be before he can answer. Residents are kept pretty busy. But she's in the best place, and it's a good hospital."

Ronica glanced back and saw that Keisha had a comforting hand on Natalie's arm.

"Yeah," Natalie said. "You're right."

Ronica knew exactly where the hospital was located, having made the journey several times from Forgotten over the years, the last time being when Fletcher had been found sleeping in his beloved alfalfa fields and almost died.

Xander didn't text Keisha, but he did call and ask to talk to Natalie. She listened intently and then thanked him before hanging up.

"Well?" Ronica asked, looking at her in the rearview mirror.

"It's her liver. It's failing. She couldn't breathe, and they intubated her. That's what Caleb hasn't told me and why they've got her sedated. They don't know if she'll regain consciousness."

"Oh, Natalie. I'm so sorry." Ronica pressed on the gas a little harder.

Olivia stirred. "Is something wrong?"

"No, just rest," Ronica told her. "Unless . . . do you feel like you can eat? We could stop and get you something from your bag."

"When I get home," she said. "Keisha can make me another one of Natalie's smoothies." She twisted her head to look at her niece. "If that's okay."

"Sure. I saw how she made it," Keisha said, sounding odd. Ronica understood why because she'd also never heard Olivia ask so nicely for anything.

They drove the rest of the way in silence, and after they arrived at the hospital, Keisha gave Natalie a hug before taking the wheel. "I'll be praying," she said.

"Thank you," Natalie whispered.

Ronica walked arm-in-arm with her friend into the hospital. Natalie's steps were slower now as if she didn't want to reach her destination.

"I'll be right here if you need me," Ronica said when they reached the ICU waiting room.

"What if . . . what if this is the end? We didn't have time to make up . . . I don't . . . I can't . . ."

"Yes, you can," Ronica said firmly. "Go to your husband. He needs you too." She gave her friend a push through the door.

Natalie was in a daze. Joni lay in the hospital bed, her blue-dyed hair dull against the white pillowcase. Her skin looked as if someone had rubbed in a tanning solution that had gone a terrible yellow, and her face was skeletal, almost unrecognizable. Her stomach, however, was hugely distended, which was apparently the reason for the intubation and the struggle to breathe. Not only was her liver failing, but also her kidneys. Everything else seemed to be shutting down in response.

Caleb was arguing with the doctor about a liver transplant, volunteering to give a piece of his own. The doctor kept shaking his head. "I'm sorry. Your daughter is an alcoholic, and she isn't eligible."

"Why?" Natalie demanded. "If one of us is willing to donate part of our liver and pay for the operation, what do you care?" They might not have all the money yet, but the entire town of Forgotten would stand behind them. She was sure of it.

Compassion shone from the doctor's eyes. "Currently, she isn't strong enough to endure a transplant. But even if she was, these cases go before the board, and they won't approve it because the odds aren't good that she will be able to beat the addiction. I'm really sorry, but that's the truth."

The air in the room seemed to have vanished, and Natalie struggled for breath. "Oh, God," she prayed. Caleb put an arm around her, anchoring her as her knees started to crumble.

"But she's here now," she said to the doctor, finding strength she didn't know she had. "Couldn't she get better?"

"Unfortunately, her kidneys are also affected, and that's why her chest is so swollen. That's all water. We can tap the water from her lungs, and it will ease the pressure so maybe we can take her off the vent, but taking the water could cause complications."

"So what can we do?" Natalie pressed, gripping her husband's arm tightly.

"We give it some time and see what the next round of tests brings. But you need to prepare yourselves because at the moment your daughter has less than a five percent chance of recovery. The next day or two will tell us more." He hesitated before adding, "It may be that you will need to make the decision about whether or not to take her off the vent and let nature take its course."

"No!" Natalie shook her head emphatically. "No, just no."

"Okay. Right. We're not there yet, and we'll do everything we can." With another sympathetic nod, the doctor started toward the door but then paused. "You might, however, call any other family members, especially any children."

"She doesn't have children."

"Oh." He looked puzzled. "I see."

Before he could turn away again, Natalie asked, "Why would you think that she did?"

"During our examination, one of the nurses reported seeing stretchmarks that are typical for women who've given birth."

"You think she might have had a baby recently?" Natalie asked, too stunned to know how to feel.

"No, these are older marks. They never really heal." He glanced toward the bed. "And with her current nutritional state, it's very unlikely that she is menstruating, and even less likely she'd be able to sustain a pregnancy. Since she wasn't awake when she was brought in, we couldn't get any information, and we made an assumption. We can update the file."

"No." Natalie shook her head. "She . . . we don't know. Maybe she did have a child." Before, when she'd disappeared. But if that had been the case, why hadn't Joni told them when she came back?

The doctor nodded and left, visibly relieved to go.

Natalie looked at her husband. "What do you think?"

"I don't know." His voice was hoarse.

Natalie took a step toward the bed, reaching out to touch Joni's hand. "How did this happen?" she asked. "How did we not know about this problem when she still listened to us . . . when we might have been able to help?"

"I guess she was hiding it from us," Caleb said. Normally, her husband was a big, tall, red-faced man with all the confidence in the world, but right now he looked gray and beaten. "Don't blame yourself. We couldn't have known."

Natalie bit her lip so hard it drew blood. "I think I knew it wasn't just digestive problems. She was wasting away in front of us." She burst into tears.

Caleb pulled her close. "It's not your fault. She's an adult. We did our best. We did."

Even last week, she might have pushed him away and denied his words, taking the blame like a cross on her back, but a week in the online estranged parent group and last night's meeting had changed her. Joni was an adult, and she had made her choices. They had done their best as parents. They'd rescued her every time she'd been in need, called her Angelica or whatever name she was currently using, and loved her with their whole hearts.

"We'll have to get her into therapy," she muttered into his chest, pushing away the heartache that threatened to smother her.

Caleb rested his chin on her head. "Five percent chance," he reminded her.

"I know, but as long as she's breathing and her brain is working, there is still hope." This hope was every bit as terrible as waiting for Joni to contact her, but she was going to embrace it just the same. "And did you call Kenley? She needs to know."

"I called her last night after I got here and saw how swollen she was and how odd the nurses were acting. She's on her way."

That eased Natalie's pain a tiny bit. "Okay then. But for the record, you should have told me how bad it was."

"Hey, Ronica!"

At the call, Ronica looked up to see Doc and Carina Sayers coming into the waiting room. Their daughter, Amara, was with them, as she normally was, clutching her stuffed blue alicorn.

Ronica stood, smiling and waving at the child before saying, "I'm glad to see you guys. Natalie went inside, and I've heard nothing since. I'm worried about her."

Doc nodded gravely. "I'll go in and talk to them."

"The nurses will let you in?" Ronica asked.

"I have practicing rights in this hospital, and I'm also Joni's family doctor, even if I haven't seen her for the past few years. I delivered her, you know."

"Yeah, I know," Ronica said. "Her and half the residents of Forgotten."

"I'll wait here," Carina said to her husband in lyrical, accented English. To her daughter, she added something in quiet Spanish, and the little girl waved at her dad before following her mother to a chair next to Ronica.

"Davy is really concerned about Joni—Angelica, I mean," Carina told Ronica, calling her husband by his real name instead of Doc like the rest of the town. "He talked to Xander this morning, and it's not looking good." She sighed. "Poor thing. She came to the clinic several times over the years, you know. She told him things—things he still won't tell me. He said he tried to help her, even to the point of getting her into a recovery clinic or something earlier last year, but now he feels a lot of guilt for not doing more."

"Don't we all." Ronica narrowed her eyes. "Xander doesn't think she's going to make it, does he? He wouldn't say as much when Natalie talked to him, but I think she could tell."

"No. They don't think she will," Carina agreed.

They sat in silence, with Ronica wondering what she could do. One minute everything was normal, and the next, the world had exploded into uncertainty for too many people she loved.

"You should go home." Carina's gaze probed her face. "You look a little beat, which is understandable after the week you've had."

Ronica forced a chuckle. "I don't have a car at the moment. We were driving Olivia to a medical appointment when this happened."

"We can give you a ride after we finish our errands here."

Ronica noticed Carina didn't ask for details about Olivia. Maybe as a doctor's wife, she was accustomed to not probing. "Thanks. I'll think about it. I might go to one of my children's, but I'm worried Natalie might need me. Things haven't been great between Natalie and Joni, and now this. I just wish both Natalie's children would have come to see her more."

"Well, they do have their own lives," Carina said. "My boys keep talking about graduating and moving far away to go to college or some other adventure—some of them dangerous adventures, mind you. Like backpacking through the Amazon or sea diving in some country whose name not even I can pronounce. They think they'll live forever and that there is always plenty of time." She chuckled. "If it weren't for Amara, I might lose it when they graduate."

Amara smiled and left the drawing she was making to wrap her arms around her mother's neck. "I love you, Mommy."

Carina kissed her. "I love you too, sweetie."

"And how are you doing?" Ronica asked her. When the Sayers had opened their home to her as a newborn, they hadn't known how severe her congenital scoliosis might be, and though so far Amara had not needed surgical intervention, Carina said it was becoming increasingly apparent that she would need some kind of help in the future.

"I'm good," Amara said, ducking her head.

"She may need a brace." Carina smoothed her daughter's hair. "We're still watching and waiting. In the meantime, we're doing specific exercises for her curve, but nothing too radical. Whatever it is, we will face it together. Right, honey?"

"Uh-huh." Amara moved back to her drawing.

Ronica watched her for a moment, and then Carina said, "I hear we have a wedding coming—and really soon."

Unexpected joy spread through Ronica. "That's right. I'm so excited. I'm doing all the decorations for the reception room at City Hall. It used to be a ballroom, you know."

"I didn't, but it's certainly elegant enough. It's a wonderful place for a Valentine's Day wedding. And you deserve it." Carina touched her hand with a little squeeze.

For some reason that made Ronica think of Josiah and how he could have been her plus-one at the wedding. Yet she couldn't find it in herself to hate Olivia for that, not with what she was going through.

"I can text you when we are ready to head home," Carina offered.

Ronica shook her head. "If I know Natalie, she won't leave Joni here alone, and she might need support. Now that I don't have Fletcher to look after . . ." No pain accompanied the observation, but Ronica stopped all the same. "I'll probably stay."

"I understand. If you change your mind, shoot me a text."

Doc Sayer hadn't yet returned when Kenley McColl came flying into the waiting room, wearing a dark suit, her blond hair in a ponytail. She recognized them immediately. "Am I in the right place?" she asked as they rose to meet her. "I drove all night after my dad called. Is there any news about my sister?"

Ronica shook her head. "We haven't heard anything since your mom went inside the ICU, but we can let her know you're here."

"I'll text her." Kenley's phone was already in her hand.

"They only allow two people back in the room," Carina said. "Sometimes they'll make an exception though, if . . ." She glanced at Ronica, who understood what she wasn't saying—if they didn't think the person was going to make it.

"Oh, right." Kenley nodded without looking at them. "She's coming out. Apparently, Doc's with them looking at all the test results. That's good to know." She gave a tight smile to Carina. "Your husband's the best doctor I've ever had, which is why I make an appointment every time I visit my parents."

They didn't have to wait long before Natalie came out, looking stronger than when she'd gone in, which surprised Ronica until she remembered the way she'd been around her own children after Fletcher began to deteriorate more rapidly.

"Kenley!" She stretched upward to tightly hug her much taller daughter as if she'd never let her go. "I'm glad you got here safely."

"Joni? Is she awake?"

Natalie drew back, shaking her head. "Her liver is failing. Kidneys too. The doctors are not hopeful."

"So, does that mean . . .?" Tears came to Kenley's eyes, but they didn't fall, and when she continued, her voice was tightly controlled. "She can have part of my liver. That's a thing, right? And a kidney too."

"Her kidneys are only failing because of the liver, not because they're bad, and she's not a candidate for transplant because she's too weak and because of the alcohol."

"What? She's drinking again?"

"Again?" Natalie gaped at her daughter. "You knew?"

"She had a problem after high school," Kenley said with a shrug. "I told her to get help. She said she would. And I'm sure she did because she asked me to drive her to a free recovery clinic."

Natalie studied her for a few moments. "She *wanted* to go?"

"Yeah. She said she wanted a new life. I thought . . ." Kenley pursed her lips. "She was dating some guy, and she thought he might marry her. She even showed me the money he gave her. A lot of it." She shook her head. "But a few months later, she showed up at my apartment and asked to spend a few nights. They'd broken up. But I told you about that. It was during that second time she stopped calling you."

"Was she drunk when she showed up at your apartment?"

"I can't say for sure. But I don't think so."

Natalie nodded, glancing at Ronica and Carina, though Ronica didn't know if Natalie registered their presence before turning back to Kenley. "Do you know anything about a pregnancy?" Natalie asked.

"What? No!" Kenley's face contracted with either surprise or horror. Ronica couldn't say which.

Natalie's narrow shoulders wilted. "The doctor says she might have been pregnant because she has stretch marks. Not recent ones, though. Could have been anytime that we didn't see her for a while."

"I don't know anything about it," Kenley began. "But . . ."

Natalie pounced. "But what?"

"Well, when I drove her to the clinic, I thought it was weird that she was wearing so much clothing, and her face was . . . well, she's always been so thin, but she looked normal, like she'd been eating more than just vegetables for a change." She sighed. "But, Mom, even if she was, she probably didn't go through with the pregnancy. So I'm not sure what . . ." Kenley stepped closer to Natalie, wrapping her arms around her. "Maybe we should concentrate on getting her better."

"You're right." Natalie seemed to wilt under her daughter's strength. "You can come in with me. I checked. I just wanted to ask you about Joni first, and I wanted to tell Ronica—" She looked past her to where Ronica waited. "Thank you so much for staying, but you can go home. We're going to be awhile."

"I'll stick around for a bit," Ronica said. "When you need me to, I'll bring food. And I can go to your place and pick up anything you want and bring it back, okay?" She'd borrow her daughter's car if necessary.

"I couldn't ask you to do that."

"Your place is only twenty minutes from here. Go on back. And let me know."

"Thanks," Natalie said so softly that Ronica mostly read her lips.

When they were gone, Carina met Ronica's eyes, her expression thoughtful. "I didn't get stretch marks until I was eight months along," she said.

Ronica nodded. "I got them at seven months with Violet. And a lot more at six months with the twins. So if Joni has them . . ."

"She might have a child out there."

Ronica held Carina's gaze, not knowing if this would bring Natalie more pain or a bit of peace. Either way, she knew she had to try to uncover the truth to help her friend.

CHAPTER 14

Josiah sat in his office Saturday morning, trying to clear away some of the work that had piled up this week, mainly due to his own distraction. Being in his home office, the one place in his family home that had remained untouched by Olivia's constant updating, made him feel comfortable and nostalgic as he sat among items that had belonged to both his father and grandfather. There was a sense of permanence here. It was only when he left the office that the feeling of being in someone else's house overtook him, and he knew the feeling would intensify the moment Olivia stepped back into the house.

Olivia, who was dying and who expected too much. Still, he couldn't help feeling sorry for her, so he'd come home—or at least to the guest room closest to Charlie's bedroom. This week she'd turned on the charm, flirting and acting as though they hadn't almost divorced. Disbelief at her audacity had stilled his responses, both good and bad. The feeling that he was living someone else's life was a persistent thought.

He hadn't brought much back from the mayoral residence, and

instead had been stopping there each morning to shower and change after dropping Charlie off at school. There was plenty of time to get to work after, now that he wasn't driving to the reservoir to pick up Charlie or spending so much of his free time helping Ronica with Fletcher.

Josiah had asked his son how he was feeling that morning before dropping him off at the vet clinic—without, he hoped, hinting at his conversation with Ronica—and Charlie had seemed relieved to have a discussion. It turned out he'd noticed the lack of clothing changes and the way Josiah kept to himself at the house. He'd worried about the too-polite conversations between his parents as they shared family dinners made by a stranger.

Josiah hadn't meant to act differently, but he'd never felt so . . . so devastated. He'd come back from the betrayal to a point where he could envision a future with a woman he loved and who would be faithful, and every day apart from her was a life sentence in a prison with bars of guilt.

No wonder Charlie worried about him.

They planned some ice fishing, though it was the last thing Josiah wanted to do because they'd taken Fletcher with them three weeks ago, and seeing Fletcher under the ice was something he wouldn't easily forget. But Charlie was excited, and Josiah decided he would bring more of his belongings back to the Lake House and invite Charlie and Olivia to actually make a meal together tomorrow.

What to do about Olivia and her flirting, he didn't know. It made him unsettled because she was still a very attractive woman, and he was a man after all. But so much flirting made him wonder if she was exaggerating her case the way she often exaggerated other situations in the past when trying to force him to do something. The suspicion ate at him. Over the years, he'd learned to see through her subterfuge, but not always perfectly, and it bothered him that he cared whether or not she was lying. Yet again.

When Olivia wanted to impress, she was a bright, shining star that attracted every eye and enticed worship. But he'd already ridden that horse to the ground. He understood that deep down, the only person Olivia cared for was herself. Even Charlie was in part an appendage that checked one of the boxes she'd made for her life—otherwise, she'd accept and protect his dreams instead of trying to replace them with her own.

Okay, so he'd have a talk with her doctors to be sure the documents she'd shown him were accurate. But would it make a difference? Maybe. All he knew was that right now he felt a heavy, constant weight of anxiety on his chest that seemed permanent.

Ridiculous. He hated feeling so weak or allowing his wife to have that effect on him. All he wanted was to call Ronica, if only to hear her voice, but he knew she was at the hospital with Natalie, and she didn't need to know about his concerns, not when he'd chosen to stay with Olivia.

He had no right.

A door somewhere in the house shut, and Josiah realized he'd read to the end of the document in his hand without internalizing a single word. The door had to be Olivia getting home, driven by Keisha, who would now need a ride back to her apartment. He rose, glad for the distraction.

Keisha met him in the hallway outside his office, and he felt guilty at his relief that Olivia wasn't with her.

"She went up to her room," Keisha said, seeing his glance past her. "I came to ask you for a ride home." She leaned inward and upward to give him a hug.

"Be glad to." If there was anything besides Charlie that Josiah was grateful to Olivia for, it was his relationship with Keisha. They weren't blood, but he was her uncle in every sense of the word.

She pulled back, examining his face. "I'm sorry about the cancer. This is probably the worst thing that could have happened. Not just to Olivia but to you too."

He shook his head. "Charlie is healthy," he said. *And Ronica,* he added silently. "He's the most important thing."

Keisha nodded. "So, um, the treatment yesterday and today? I don't think they went well at all." She glanced upward in the direction of the master suite. "I mean, she didn't say much, but maybe they can measure what happens on the first day and extrapolate what might happen after that."

"The second treatment wasn't planned?"

She shook her head. "I think there may be more than I'm guessing." She paused a moment. "I've never seen Olivia this way before. Not ever."

That prompted a strangled snort from Josiah. "Yeah. She's struggling."

"And you?" Her stare sharpened.

He thought about that. "I've been struggling almost since the day we married."

"Yeah." Keisha nodded. "But this time . . . Look, I'm moving my wedding to early March. Xander can take a week off then, and that way . . . I'm letting Olivia have free reign with the wedding—well, with the stipulation that it's held in Forgotten. My parents left me a fund to pay for it, and I might as well let her . . . I'm the closest thing she'll ever have to a daughter."

"She might still recover." His tongue felt thick.

"No, she won't. Today she asked me to be her executor. She's putting everything into a trust for Charlie. I know you said it might be years, but I don't think so."

A wave of dizziness passed over him. So it was true. Olivia wasn't lying about the gravity of her illness. He shook his head to clear it and saw tears starting down Keisha's face. He pulled himself together enough to ask, "How are you holding up?"

"I've hated her so much these past months, and even before that she was, well, difficult. But after my parents died . . . I'll never repay either of you for giving me a home and family."

He pulled her into another hug. "Ah, that was the simple part. You are easy to love, and I will always be your uncle, no matter what." Actually, these days he felt more like her father because he was so proud of her.

She grinned up at him, her eyes bright with tears. "Good, because I need you to walk me down the aisle."

He tilted his head forward in a little bow. "I would be honored."

"Good." She turned. "Okay, now give me that ride home."

Josiah returned to the house, and this time it not only felt like a stranger's place, but it also felt too quiet and still. *Like death,* he thought.

He took the stairs two at a time and sprinted to the master suite. At the last second, he knocked on the door a little too vigorously.

No answer.

"Olivia," he called. "It's me."

He heard something then. Mumbling, and then a faint, "Come in."

For the second time that day he felt relief, but this time because she was there. Not dead.

She was in bed, though, where he found her sitting with her laptop and several books, one of which looked like a journal. She looked decidedly worse than when he'd last seen her yesterday morning before he shoveled the drive and drove Charlie to school. Maybe it was a reaction to the radiation treatments, the continued chemo, or even the driving, but she appeared weaker—and somehow more lovely than ever. But then, her looks were never the problem.

"Are you okay?" he asked.

She lifted her eyes, holding his gaze. He could see on her face that she didn't want to tell him. "Please," he said.

A tiny smile appeared around her full lips.

"What?" he asked.

"Your voice. It was the first thing I noticed about you. Well, that and the way you dug into that ravioli at Gandolf's when no one else would touch it."

For the first time in what felt like weeks, his chuckle was real. He sat on the edge of the bed. "Well, I'd had a long day on the ranch since some of my hands quit, and that was the only thing I'd eaten since that morning."

"We had some good times." She leaned back, somehow looking stronger. Maybe having family around her was what she needed.

"So you survived the night at the short-term rental."

"Yes."

"And the treatment?"

Her expression stilled. "Not working as well as they'd hoped. With the concentrated dose, they should have seen at least some reaction right away. I'll go back next week to monitor it again, but . . . it's not promising. No better than the last time."

"I'm sorry." He didn't know how to feel about this information.

"I know you are. Everybody is." She smiled again, but this time the emotion didn't reach her eyes. "And the ladies—especially Ronica and Natalie—are so nice. Too nice. Interfering."

"Are you saying you don't want them to go with you anymore?" This didn't surprise him. He'd have to go instead. Maybe he could take a leave of absence because he didn't see any way to be gone that much from his office. And what about Charlie? The last thing he wanted was to uproot his son to move near the cancer center.

"That's exactly what I'm saying. But it's not what you think." She sighed. "I realize that I don't deserve their care, and especially not from Ronica."

"What do you mean?" A lump formed in his throat, throttling the words.

"I mean because I'm the one standing between what you both want." She shook her head, her smile now mocking. "I know how you feel about her, and I can see how she feels about you. And you know, it's almost too easy to take advantage of your . . . your honor. Both of you."

Josiah swallowed hard, but the lump remained. Was this the moment she asked for something more? What more did he have that he hadn't already agreed to give to her . . . except this house and full custody of Charlie?

"Don't look at me like that." Her tone hardened. She spun the laptop around and showed him the screen. "I've signed the papers. You're free."

"But . . . I don't understand."

She lowered her gaze, her lashes hiding her eyes completely. "I heard Ronica talking to you about Charlie. That he's worried about you. And I realized he has a right to be. You had started to be yourself again, even with me—even while we fought about the house and everything else related to the divorce. You were firm and bold in your fight for Charlie, yet giving and fair to me. You were the man I fell in love with. At least until I made you come back."

"You didn't make me do anything."

"Yes. I did." She looked up at him again, her eyes seeming to peer into his soul. "I used your honor against you. You are always going to want to take care of your family and everyone else. Ronica Wilson is the same way. But you taking care of me is over as far as I'm concerned. I will be moving to Lincoln while I complete my treatment, whatever that means."

"Alone?" he asked. At the moment, she looked barely able to sit up.

"No. My second cousin will be coming to stay with me in an apartment. I'll be paying her a good share of my grandparents' trust fund. There will be a room for Charlie, but I don't want him to see this every day." She pointed to her head. "Especially when I'm having the worst effects. And truth be told, I don't want you to see me this way either."

That was news to him. Her being sick was a lot less ugly than learning she'd cheated on him.

"Charlie needs to get used to not having me around," she continued. "But you must promise to bring him every weekend for as long as I'm able to have him. Can you do that?"

He nodded. "If it makes you feel better, I'll have my attorney draw up an addendum to our custody arrangement."

She hesitated before responding, and he knew she wanted to agree, but she finally shook her head. "No need. I trust you, Josiah."

Trust. How odd that she should trust him because trust was something he would never again have for her.

"I'll pay to extend my health insurance," she continued, "and after that time is up . . . well, I don't think it will matter by then. I'll either be going one way or the other." She frowned. "Why are you looking at me like that?"

"It's just . . ." He chose his words carefully. "This isn't like you."

"What, you don't think cancer has changed me?"

He knew better than to step into that.

She waved a hand as if dismissing the answer he didn't give. "Well, it has some, but my motives aren't completely altruistic." She gave a little roll of her eyes. "The bottom line is that I may not have the years I was hoping for, and this means you are all I have left to help Charlie remember me. But I don't have time to win you over again to my side, especially when I am so tired and you are so obviously in love with someone else." She held her hand up to stop the words that came to his mouth. "I know it's largely my fault, and you have every right to be angry with me. And *that* is my sole motive. I don't want your words about me to Charlie to be clouded by more anger than you already feel toward me."

Ah, so there was the catch. There always was one with Olivia.

"Do you think you can remember the good times for him?" she asked. "Do you think you can turn aside your anger at me?"

Could he keep her good memories alive for Charlie? Would her last action of freeing them both make up for all that came before? He simply didn't know. But she was trying, and so could he.

"I'm not angry with you," he said finally.

"Yes, you are. You might even hate me. But maybe now that I've set you free, we can become friends again."

Now that the marriage was over, she meant, when they didn't have to live together or worry about petty things like infidelity and pride. How odd to expect to finally become friends after divorce, when they hadn't gotten it right with seventeen years of marriage. But maybe for them it would work.

"Okay," he said simply. "I'll do my best to speak positively of you. Now, what else can I do to help?"

Her lips twitched with a smile that didn't fully materialize. "Nothing at the moment. I need to rest today, and my second cousin will arrive tomorrow. She'll help me figure out what to take. Maybe you can keep Charlie at the mayoral residence tomorrow until I'm gone. I think it might be stressful for him to see me getting ready to leave."

What she didn't say, but what he understood, was that she didn't think she'd be coming back. Not ever. So she'd be taking most of her personal belongings and probably some of the furniture as well.

"All right," he agreed. "Let me know if you need anything."

"Right now I just want to sleep."

"What about something to eat?"

"I'm having Maggie bring food over from the café. Maybe send her up when she comes?"

"Okay, I will."

She brought a hand to the base of her scalp behind her ear, pushing on her wig gently and then grimacing. She probably wanted to remove it, but she wouldn't do that as long as he was in the room.

"I'll be downstairs if you need anything." He pivoted and strode across the oh-so-plush carpet.

He'd already reached the door when she called out, "Oh, and

Josiah, you're not getting any younger. You should really propose sooner rather than later."

He blinked. "Um, Fletcher has barely died." He winced as the words came of their own volition.

She gave a snort. "There you go with the honor again. Fletcher has been gone a long, long time. We both know that."

Josiah left her without responding, but for the first time in days, he felt life seeping back into him. No, not life, but hope. Hope that he could find happiness and still meet his gaze in the mirror every morning. Olivia had signed the papers, and his attorney would file them electronically. There weren't all that many divorces happening in Forgotten, so maybe by the end of Monday, if he pulled a string or two, he'd be free.

He'd always seen divorce as a failure, but the idea of being free from Olivia made him feel like a man again. He had to tell Ronica as soon as possible. What would she say?

What would Fletcher say?

But he already knew.

CHAPTER 15

Ronica's daughter, Violet, came with her two children to visit Ronica and eat lunch at the hospital cafeteria. She offered to stay for a while, but Ronica knew Violet had her hands full at home, so she arranged for them to pick her up later to spend the night at Violet's. Ronica probably should go back to Forgotten, but she was too worried about Natalie.

After they left, Ronica brought lunch up for the family, and they came out to the waiting room to eat, taking turns so as not to leave Joni alone. By then, several other families had gathered in the ICU waiting room, so Ronica headed downstairs to a more private place on the main floor to begin her research on Joni's possible pregnancy. From where she sat on her bench in the hallway, she could see people arriving through the main entry, many of the visitors carrying balloons or flowers. Some walked briskly while others dragged their steps and curled in on themselves. One tall, painfully thin teenage boy with a backpack headed slowly to the elevator that led to the ICU. He wore only ragged pants and a stretched-out sweater against the cold, and his limp made him look like he should be the one in the hospital. Then the doors shut him inside, and he was gone.

Ronica refocused on her phone. With the information she'd received from Kenley about the recovery clinic where she'd dropped off her sister five years ago, Ronica didn't have any trouble finding the number to call. But tracking down information about Joni—or Angelica, as the people at the clinic called her—turned out to be more difficult. Due to privacy issues, the three different women she talked to at the clinic confirmed very little. If the patient were to sign a waiver, they said, or if she were unconscious and in critical condition, the next of kin could at least get information that might be relevant. The last woman told Ronica she doubted the information they had would be useful to Angelica's current situation.

"It's just because of the child," Ronica said, making her voice sound casual, as if she knew all about a baby. "We haven't been able to locate the child."

"Well, as I said, I don't believe the information we have here can help. We don't know what happened after her time here. Please have her parents contact us with the appropriate requests."

To Ronica, the response seemed to indicate that there might have been a baby or at least a pregnancy on those records. Maybe she could go there with Natalie to ask more, but if the information couldn't help Joni's current condition, then the clinic would probably deny their request anyway. Unless Joni passed away, though Ronica didn't want to consider that just yet.

Next, using contacts she'd made during Fletcher's illness, she managed to find the location where the ambulance picked Joni up last night. It was on the border of a tiny blink-and-you'll-miss-it town west of Panna Creek. All this time while Natalie had agonized over the estrangement with her daughter, she'd been that close.

She arranged an Uber out to the location, where she found a rundown shack in the middle of some trees. A huge black dog was tied in the yard, and he barked like a thing possessed, but no one came to the door, and she couldn't pass the animal to knock, so the driver took her back to town. Maybe she'd return later with Caleb and some of his friends from the local police department.

She was further deflated by a message from Kenley about Joni having a seizure. *They're doing tests now,* Kenley texted. *It looks bad. The nurses are avoiding eye contact.*

Please let me know if there's anything I can do, Ronica wrote back.

She was eating dinner in the hospital cafeteria when she noticed the boy she'd seen enter the hospital earlier. Well, not actually a boy, it turned out, though he had the lanky figure of a teen. He was too thin, with bad skin and longish brown hair that might not have been washed in weeks. His clothes were large, his worn pants hanging on him with a belt, and the backpack was dirty and ragged. She saw him staring at the menu, then looking in his wallet and frowning. He carried with him a bag from the gift shop with something big inside. A stuffed animal maybe.

She left her tray in the nearly deserted cafeteria and went toward him. "Hi," she said.

He looked at her quickly, then glanced down and away. "Hi."

"Tough day?"

"Yeah." He looked at her again, longer this time. His light blue eyes were bloodshot, but he was present in the moment, not high or hungover from what she could tell.

"Same," she said. "My good friend's daughter is in the ICU with liver failure, and she just had a seizure. I'm waiting for more information."

"Me too." He paused before adding, "Well, not the seizure, but the waiting. It's my girlfriend, Jazzy. I don't know if she's going to be okay."

"I'm sorry. Why don't you order and come sit with me?"

He looked again at the menu board. "I don't have . . . I'd better go ask if they'll let me see her. They were waiting on tests before and couldn't check about me going in." He looked down at the bag. "I found something to cheer her up."

"She's in good hands," Ronica said. "Please, order something. It's on me."

He blinked and looked up at the board again before returning his gaze to her face. "You don't have to—"

"I insist. I'd love the company. I'm Ronica, by the way. Ronica Wilson."

"Nolan Holt."

"Nice to meet you. What would you like, Nolan?"

Her offer proved too much for him to resist. He ordered a vegan hamburger, fries, and drink combo, and she added a strawberry shake and two orders of gooey butter cake. It wouldn't be as good as Maggie's, but she doubted this man-boy would notice.

They sat at the table, Ronica finishing her salad while he inhaled his entire hamburger in about four bites. She should have gotten him two. As he dug into the fries, she pushed the shake and one of the pieces of cake over to him. "These are for you too."

"Really?"

"Hope you like strawberry." She hadn't asked him for his flavor preference because she hadn't wanted to seem too pushy about buying the extra items.

"I'm good with everything. Thanks." He continued to eat but with less intensity now.

Ronica wondered where his parents were. It would kill her to see any of her adult sons looking like this and being here all alone when he was obviously distraught and out of money.

"So, do you live around here?"

He nodded. "Yeah."

That wasn't much. "I'm from Forgotten. Have you ever been there?"

"No, I'm originally from Kansas City. I've only been here a few months."

"Your family lives there?"

He hesitated. "I got a brother there. My parents retired to Florida."

"That's a long way."

"Yeah. We don't really talk."

"What about your girlfriend?"

"Her parents are dead." His eyes widened. "Sorry. I mean, they've passed."

"But she's from here?"

"Lincoln, I think." He took a long drink of the shake. "And she's not really my girlfriend. I mean, we're together right now, but she's kind of out of my league, you know? I'm just glad to be with her for as long as she'll have me." There was hurt in the words. "I guess I hope she'll come around."

The relationship didn't sound all that great if he knew that she was only biding her time until something better came along. "What happened?"

"I don't know. She just collapsed. She hasn't been feeling well."

"Could she be expecting?"

That got a grin from him. "I wish, though I don't know how we'd pay for that. But no, I don't think she can have children. Anyway, I'm careful."

They went back to eating as Ronica kept the conversation going, mostly about the hospital and the food.

Thinking of Natalie and her estrangement, she said, "Do you talk with your parents?"

"I text on holidays." He frowned. "I don't think . . . I'm just not . . . they aren't really proud of me. My brother is the one with the good job, beautiful wife, and three kids."

"What do you do?"

He shrugged. "Whatever comes around. Working for a builder at the moment, but there's not much going on in the winter. It's temporary work."

Ronica didn't feel she could push further. He was a little like a stray dog—grateful, wary, and a bit intimidating. She wouldn't worry about him in an alley, but she wouldn't leave her purse near him.

They finished eating at the same time and found themselves on the same path up to the waiting room of the ICU. She checked her phone, but there was no news from Kenley or Natalie. Ronica resisted the urge to text for an update. They knew she was out here if they needed her, but the last thing she wanted was for them to concern themselves with her wellbeing. She had a bunch of texts from her daughter, and Laina and Jeremy as well, but she had no new information to give them since the seizure. All she could do was pray.

Nolan had talked on the phone to someone at the ICU, but they didn't let him in. Dejectedly, he turned from the door, and she waved at him. He came to sit by her, unslinging his backpack and setting it on the floor. He kept the bag with the stuffed animal on his lap.

"They won't let me in," he told her. "I don't know why. They're saying I'm not family, but I'm all Jazzy's got."

"What's her last name? Her first name is unusual enough that we should be able to find a connection."

He frowned. "Bright. But it's not her real name. Neither is Jazzy. Maybe that's why they won't tell me anything."

"You don't know her real name?"

He shrugged. "A lot of our friends change their names. Not me. Mostly the girls. We've only been together four months. I saw her license once, but I . . . well, we were partying, and I don't remember the name. The ambulance people found it last night in her purse."

"And she has no family?"

"Yeah, a sister. They aren't close, though."

"Do you know the sister's number? Or her name? Maybe where she lives?"

He thought for a moment, then reached for his backpack. "No, but I have Jazzy's phone. I bet the number's in there. I don't have the passcode, though. She always uses her fingerprint. But I know the code has a five and a two in it."

The iPhone in a beautiful bright blue case looked like a newer one, though the screen cover was cracked. He lifted his gaze to Ronica. "You think I ought to try?"

"Yeah." She supposed the hospital personnel might have already called the sister, if they had her actual name, but she could see Nolan was eager to do something to help his girlfriend. "But are those the first two numbers?"

"Pretty sure the five is first. Or maybe the second. I don't know about the rest." He tried several number combinations and was locked out. "It says I can try again in fifteen minutes. But I think it will lock me out permanently if I do too many more." He sighed and started to turn off the phone, but Ronica pointed at the picture on the lock screen. It was a stuffed animal, one that looked eerily familiar.

"What's that?" she asked, her finger still hovering in the air.

He smiled. "A unicorn with wings. There's a name for it, but I forgot. Used to be hers, but she said she gave it away. She must like it to keep the picture, so when I saw one in the gift shop, I had to buy it. Too bad it's pink instead of blue. Blue's her favorite color." He laid the phone on his lap and opened the shopping bag, pulling out a stuffed animal that was about fifteen inches tall.

"An alicorn," Ronica whispered, feeling suddenly out of breath.

"Yeah, that's it." He smiled briefly before looking at the ICU door again. "Do you know any way I can find out how Jazzy's doing? I need to know."

Ronica met his gaze. His eyes were a nice shape, and if he gained thirty pounds, he'd probably be attractive. Now he just looked sickly. "Nolan," she said. "Do you have any pictures of your girlfriend?"

"Yeah." Putting the alicorn back into its plastic sack, he pulled out his own cell phone, thumbing through a few pictures before showing one to her.

Ronica stared hard, but she didn't recognize the closeup of the girl. Her face was full of sharp angles. Too sharp to be attractive. So maybe the alicorn didn't mean what she thought. To be sure, she asked. "Did she come to the hospital last night?"

He nodded.

"Do you live in a little house about twenty minutes west of here?"

Again the nod. "But I don't have a car. Took me a few hours to walk here today." He frowned. "I wasn't really able to come last night . . . we'd been drinking some." Shame laced the words.

"Do you have a big black dog?"

"Yeah. Why are you asking me this? Do you know something?"

"Maybe." Ronica looked back at the phone in her hands, her stomach clenching. "Maybe. Can I see more pictures?"

"Go ahead."

She scrolled through a dozen more before she saw a picture that caught her breath.

"What is it?" Nolan asked.

She tore her gaze from the phone. "Have you ever heard of the name Joni McColl? Or Angelica McColl?"

He shook his head. "No, I don't think so. Why?"

"Because I think my friend's daughter is your girlfriend."

CHAPTER 16

The on-call neurologist and his team arrived in record time with fancy portable equipment. Joni's seizure had only lasted a few terrifying seconds, but somehow it seemed to have changed everything. The nurses were softer-spoken now and did not quite meet Natalie's gaze. Not a good sign. But the breathing machine was loud in the room, and Joni's chest was still going up and down as if she might awaken at any moment.

Clinging to hope, Natalie scarcely breathed as the neurologist did his tests. When he finally turned to them, his face was devoid of emotion, as if steeling himself for what would come next.

"I'm sorry, but she's gone." He continued with more words, something about cerebral edema and intracranial hypertension, but Natalie couldn't understand the meaning. She continued to grip Joni's hand, so frail and weak and now turning cold.

"Are you sure?" she managed to ask. "There's no chance at all?"

Another doctor spoke, confirming Joni's brain death, but Natalie could hear her breathing and see her heart beating on the monitor. Her baby couldn't be gone!

Time passed as Natalie held her daughter's hand, much the way she had when she'd been sick as a child. People came and went, darkness fell outside, and still Natalie held Joni's hand.

"Mom," Kenley said as if from a great distance away. "Doc Sayer's here."

Natalie looked up into his face and knew immediately that what all the other doctors had been telling them was true. Joni was gone.

"What should we do?" she asked. Doc Sayer had delivered both her girls and had seen them through all their medical crises.

He lifted a finger to wipe tears from his lashes. "She's not there anymore. As a doctor and as your friend, I recommend that you take out the tube and let her go."

Natalie stared at him. How ironic it was that last night she'd been trying to come to terms with a way to continue her life knowing Joni didn't want any part of her, and now Joni was really gone. There had been no tearful goodbye or death-bed apology. There was no chance of future dressmaking together, pattern brainstorming, or grandchildren to kiss and hug. It was over. Really and truly over.

Caleb's hand covered hers. "Honey, can you understand? Do you need something?"

"I can prescribe some medicine," Doc offered.

Natalie actually had some pills in her purse, also prescribed by Doc Sayer after she'd nearly lost her mind at Christmas when Joni had been so notably absent. He'd given her twenty pills in all with directions to take either two or four daily, depending on her anxiety, half in the morning and half at night. It was supposed to get her through the holidays. Ten days of peace if she took two daily, and five days if she took four. But she'd guarded them even more carefully, taking a single pill only once a day and only on days when she'd been ready to scream or drive her car into the reservoir. Nearly a month had passed, and she still had nine pills. Nine days where she could dull her emotions. It never helped for long, and the next day was always worse, but it was at least something.

"I'm okay." She smoothed Joni's hand as if her daughter were only sleeping.

"About the tube. How does that work?" Caleb asked Doc. He knew she would agree. She had no choice.

Doc looked over at the neurologist, who said quietly, "You'll need to sign a waiver. Then when you're ready, we'll remove it and wait for the rest of her body to shut down."

Two more hours passed before Natalie could agree. First, she combed her daughter's dull, blue-dyed hair for the last time, teasing the knots away and braiding it carefully while Kenley and Caleb watched, mostly silent. Then they removed the tube while she and Kenley held Joni's hands. The silence after the machine was off shocked Natalie. No more breaths. Joni's chest didn't rise again. Still, her heart labored on for a while, much longer than Natalie expected, and it seemed as if her own heart beat with her daughter's, connected as they once had been in the womb. At long last, as the heart monitor started screaming, the nurse turned it off as well.

"Take as long as you need." Doc Sayer's kind expression was almost too much for Natalie to bear. "I'll pick Carina up from her cousin's and give you a bit of privacy."

"Thanks, Doc," Caleb said.

"I can call the funeral home when you're ready," the nurse interjected. "But they might not come until the morning."

"They'll come," Doc told her. "I texted them. They've already left Forgotten."

She nodded. "I'll get the paperwork sorted." Doc and the nurse withdrew, leaving them alone in the very quiet room.

"Ah, my sweet girl," Natalie whispered. Joni looked at peace, more so than Natalie had seen her even when she'd been well, back when their bond had been unbroken.

Kenley wiped tears from her face. "Do you think I could have her ring?"

"You planning to pierce your nose?" Caleb's brows drew

downward. They'd found the nose ring with the other items the nurses had gathered from Joni during her stay—clothing, large earring spacers, and three studs, one each for her lip, tongue, and belly button.

"No, not that, or any of the studs." She began removing a tiny gold ring from the hand she'd been holding. "This one."

Natalie had bought the ring for Joni's sixteenth birthday, and the fact that Joni had kept it comforted her. "The nurses must have missed it."

"It just wasn't in the way." Caleb's voice was harsh, a sure sign that he was close to breaking.

Natalie backed away from Joni and took his hand. "Yes, you can have it," she told Kenley. "I'm happy for you to have something to remember your sister by."

"Mom?" Kenley lifted her phone. "Ronica says Joni's boyfriend is out there."

"Boyfriend?" Natalie thought about that for a moment, and somehow it comforted her to know Joni hadn't been alone.

"Apparently," Kenley said. "Should I tell them about her?"

"Yes." Natalie was relieved not to have to explain about Joni's death, even to her close friend. She took a breath. "And if the boyfriend wants to come say goodbye . . ." She swallowed hard. "Let him come in."

Kenley nodded, blinking back tears. "I'll go out and get him."

The boyfriend was about Joni's age, mid-twenties, and seemed to suffer from the same malnutrition she'd developed. Upon entering the room, he began sobbing with violent convulsions, huge, wet tears dropping onto Joni's neck where he'd thrown himself. "I'm sorry. I'm sorry," he said over and over.

They let him cry out his tears until finally, he drew away from the bed. Then Natalie embraced him, smelling dirt, smoke, and body odor, but not caring in the least. He sobbed some more as she patted his back and cried with him.

At last he drew away. "I didn't know she had a family." His eyes wandered over them. "You seem . . . nice."

"My parents are the best," Kenley answered tightly. "Joni . . . Joni had issues."

"Yeah," he agreed, ducking his head. "She'd drink a fifth of vodka every day. I couldn't get her to eat much."

"A fifth of vodka?" Kenley gaped at him. "That's a lot for anyone."

"I know. And that's only what she admitted to me. It could have been more. I wish . . . I should have gotten her help." He stared for a long moment at the bed, his eyes vacant.

"It's not your fault, son," Caleb assured him. "She made her own decisions."

He nodded, his gaze landing on the plastic sack he'd placed on the bed. "Oh, that's for her. An alicorn. To replace one she had a long time ago." His expression turned desperate. "Do you want to keep it?"

Natalie couldn't speak, but Kenley took the stuffed animal and pushed it into Natalie's arms. "Sure. Thank you so much."

"What's your name?" Caleb asked, stepping closer to the boy.

"Nolan."

Natalie looked down at the alicorn as Caleb did what he did best—investigate and pursue. She was glad. Maybe this boy's parents would be luckier than they had been. The fur on the stuffed animal was so soft, the small wings full of shiny glitter. What did it remind her of? Something, but her mind felt too dazed to think straight.

"W-what should I do with her things?" Nolan asked. "I mean, she didn't have a lot, but it should be yours."

Caleb looked at her. "Natalie?"

"If there's a keepsake you would like, you should keep it," Natalie said to him. "And maybe we can look through the stuff after? It would mean a lot for us to have some of her things, especially pictures or if it relates to her childhood. Then Caleb can help donate anything you would like gone."

"That would be good. Thank you." He thumbed toward the door. "I guess I'll go now."

"It was nice to meet you," Kenley said, and Natalie was grateful for her words because on any other day she would have said them herself. "We'll be in touch."

"Oh, that reminds me." Nolan swung off his backpack, digging inside. "Here's her phone."

Natalie's breath caught in her throat. So Joni had the phone, which meant she might have received the loving messages Natalie had sent her, as well as the few begging and pleading ones. And the angry one she'd sent at Christmas. But at least the last text had been a simple *I will always love you, sweet girl.*

"I can't open it," Nolan said. "But there's pictures and stuff."

Kenley took it from him and typed in a code. The phone didn't unlock. "I guess she didn't use her old password. What about a fingerprint?" She started to move toward the bed, but Caleb shook his head.

"That would work for some phones, but I'm pretty sure hers uses both a capacitive sensor and RF to unlock," he said. "It won't be possible now." He turned out to be right, which didn't surprise Natalie. Caleb was a good police chief for a reason.

"We can see about getting in later," Natalie suggested. Kenley nodded and slipped the phone into her handbag. Natalie was grateful to let her take care of it for the time being.

The funeral home people arrived, their faces somber. Natalie had known them all her life. They'd taken care of her parents when they passed, and Caleb's as well.

"We'll take good care of her," they promised as they wheeled Joni's covered body from the room. Somehow, during the removal, the boyfriend slipped away. There were so many questions Natalie wanted to ask him, but they could wait, and she was confident her husband would know where to find him.

Natalie left the ICU with Caleb and Kenley walking on either side. She was distinctly aware of the pitying looks the nursing staff sent their way. They were accustomed to death, she knew, but they understood how it affected families only too well.

The odd thing was that even as Natalie walked toward the exit, a measure of relief filled her heart. The emotion surprised her and made her steps falter.

"Are you okay?" Caleb asked, his sad eyes worried.

"Yes." And then it came to her, the reason for the relief. Tonight she wouldn't worry if Joni was lying in a ditch somewhere. Or if she was hungry, shooting up, or hooking up with some new guy who might abuse her. She wasn't going to lie awake wondering if yet one more text of sincere apology or love might receive no response.

Closure. This was what closure felt like.

She would be able to mourn openly, and everyone would understand without silently judging her and wondering what kind of monster she must be that her daughter cut her off. She would be able to cry and scream and sleep and not feel guilty for cheating Caleb of their future together.

Losing Joni today was the second worst thing that had happened to her but being estranged had been the worst. That was the truth, stark and ugly as it was. How horrific it was that something could feel worse than death!

Even so, she didn't want Joni to be gone. In fact, she'd give anything if her daughter were still in that room breathing and ignoring her—hating her—but that couldn't happen, and now Natalie's pain had a reason the world would understand. One *she* could understand.

"Mom?" Kenley prompted.

"I'll be okay." Natalie forced a smile. "We'll all be okay. We have each other." They were a family, and they all loved Joni, even if she hadn't really been capable of loving them back.

"Do you think she had a child?" Kenley asked.

Caleb shook his head. "No."

"If she did, we may never know," Natalie said. Yet why did hope come to her heart at the words?

Maybe because she was a mother.

And even though Joni had hurt her more deeply than it seemed possible to heal from, she still loved her more than her own life.

CHAPTER 17

Nolan emerged from the ICU looking more dejected than when he went in, which was understandable. This time he wasn't carrying the sack with the alicorn. Ignoring the dirt on his clothes and the distinct body odor, Ronica hugged him.

"I'm so sorry," she murmured.

He swallowed and gulped before saying, "In case you were wondering, I gave them her phone. They don't know the password either." He sighed. "The sister looks a lot like Jazzy, and her parents seem like nice people. Why would she say they were dead?"

"Joni was troubled. Maybe it seemed easier to her."

"I guess." He was silent for a moment and then frowned. "I'm going to miss her so much."

"Of course you will. And you shouldn't be alone. What about reaching out to your parents?"

He shook his head. "They blocked me on text and social media two years ago. I don't blame them. I was a jerk. I guess I thought they wouldn't do that."

"They might welcome you back."

"I doubt it. I said some pretty awful things. I meant them at the time, but now I kinda wish I hadn't said them."

"I'm sure they'll forgive you. Believe me, I'm a mom of three sons, and there's nothing I wouldn't forgive if they apologized."

"I don't know. Once I ran into my mom at the store before they moved, and I said, 'So, you're still alive?' And she said, 'Yes.' Then I said, 'Too bad,' and flipped her off." His shoulders dropped. "She just looked at me, so sad. Like I killed her myself."

Ronica stared at him, her mouth rounding in an O. She couldn't imagine saying this to someone she hated, much less her mother. After a moment of searching for something positive in his story, she said, "Well, you've recognized that was an awful thing to say to anyone. You could write them a letter."

"Maybe." He tried to smile, but it looked more like a grimace. "They wrote me letters, and I sent them back without opening them. I didn't want to hear apologies they didn't mean."

"Why would they send letters they didn't mean?"

"I guess . . . well, on TikTok they say it's a ploy to control us."

"Okay," Ronica said. "But isn't it kind of weird to listen to people online when they don't know your life or your parents?"

"I guess so." He gave a dejected sigh.

Deciding he'd had enough self-realization for the day, Ronica asked, "Are you going to be okay?"

He nodded. "I have another roommate, and he'll keep me company. Thanks for lunch." He headed toward the elevator. As it closed on him, Ronica wondered if he would be walking back to his house or if he had arranged transportation. She wished she'd thought to ask.

She was debating running after him when Doc and Carina Sayer emerged from the second elevator, this time without their daughter Amara. "How is Natalie?" Carina asked.

"I haven't seen her since Joni passed," Ronica admitted. "I was wondering if she'll even want to see me."

"Yes," Carina said, nodding emphatically. "She will."

"I'll go see how they're doing." Doc Sayer started to turn.

"Wait," Ronica said. "I actually need to talk to you both."

The two looked at her, their faces set with helpful expressions. Maybe Ronica shouldn't ask, but she had to. "About Amara. She always carries around that blue alicorn. I was wondering—was it with her when she was left on your clinic doorstep?"

"Oh, no." Carina shook her head. "I wouldn't have let her carry it around if it had. I mean, that would be like an invitation for the birth mother to kidnap her back, and after two years of searching and uncertainty, we weren't going to let that happen. The alicorn was a gift at the town baby shower we had when she was two months old and we received temporary custody. I don't even remember who gave it to her. She got a lot of stuffed animals, but she loved that one most because of the bright blue and the rainbow mane. But why do you ask?"

"Because I just saw the same unicorn—or one very like it—on Joni's phone. Her boyfriend said it was special to her, and . . ."

Carina made the connection. "And Joni might have been pregnant around the same time Amara was born." She stepped into her husband, as if needing support, and he put an arm around her.

"Come sit down." Ronica led them to the area where she had left her purse. "We don't know anything for sure, but Joni did trust you."

"Joni was an alcoholic," Doc said thoughtfully, rubbing his wife's hand. "That would go along with Amara's ARBD scoliosis diagnosis, but many young girls are alcoholic these days."

"Amara *looks* like Joni. And like Kenley too." Carina shook her head, her eyes wide and unfocused. "Why didn't I see that before? All these years, I've believed it was someone who knew us, who knew we'd take care of her. But it's been five years, and we've heard nothing . . . If we had known Joni was pregnant, we might have guessed. But now that I know about the alicorn, it has to be Joni. I feel it in my gut."

"She might have pictures on her phone," Ronica suggested.

"I'll do a DNA test," Doc said. "It will take time to come back, but it will tell us definitively one way or another." His face had lost color, and Ronica guessed why.

Ronica smiled sympathetically. "There is no way anyone can take Amara from you now."

"Of course not." Carina dismissed the words with a wave. "I only hope it is true because she is already asking why she doesn't look like her brothers. I worry that she will always wonder and feel abandoned, even though we love her as much as we love our sons. More people to love her can only be a blessing in her life." More people like the McColls, she meant, which Ronica thought was a very healthy way to look at it.

Doc Sayer looked up as the door to the ICU opened. "Here they come."

They all stood to meet the McColl family. Natalie looked exhausted and sad, clutching the pink alicorn to her chest. Caleb held one of her hands, a gruff expression on his face, while Kenley, her arm laced through her mother's, looked dazed and subdued. Now that she knew, Ronica thought Amara did resemble Kenley.

When they met, Natalie fell into Ronica's arms. "I never thought it would end this way, and yet part of me seems to have known it all along." Her voice broke on the last words.

"As long as you understand it's not your fault," Ronica whispered, hugging her fiercely. "You did all a mother could do and more. You opened Joni's Dress Shop, supported her clothing designs, and bailed her out every time she needed you. You are not responsible for her adult choices."

"Logically, I know that," Natalie replied. "I just . . . My heart doesn't seem to agree."

Ronica held her tightly for long moments more, and when they parted, Natalie gave her a strained smile. "Thank you for being here," she whispered.

"Always."

"Natalie," Carina said, stepping close to them. "Do you remember if Joni came to Amara's baby shower? About five years ago last July?"

Natalie stared at her blankly. "I think. Yes. She'd just come back after being away a year."

"Did she bring a gift? You made the christening dress, but did she bring something separate?"

Natalie considered. "I made the white dress for the christening, and she made a blue dress with a rainbow on the front. And she bought a stuffed animal, I think."

"An alicorn," Carina suggested. "Natalie, I don't want to get your hopes up, but I think our daughter, Amara, is also your grandbaby."

CHAPTER 18

Early Monday evening, Jeremy and Laina came to pick Ronica up in Panna Creek after she'd spent Saturday and Sunday nights at Violet's. She'd stayed two nights instead of one because she dreaded coming home to the silent house and the knowledge that Josiah was with Olivia. Her grandchildren were a great distraction, for which Ronica was extremely grateful.

On the way back to Forgotten, she and Laina discussed wedding plans and also the knowledge that Amara Sayer might actually be Natalie and Caleb's granddaughter. "I'm betting it's true," Laina said. "Every time I see Amara, I keep thinking she looks familiar. But Joni hasn't been around much these past five years, so I guess she didn't come to mind."

Jeremy sighed. "It's hard to believe Joni's dead."

"But not surprising," Laina put in with a frown. "Xander told Keisha that alcoholic women often have their livers fail sooner than a man who drinks a similar amount, and even in high school Joni was a drinker. It's still really sad. Her whole life is over, and what did she leave behind beside heartache for her family?"

"Maybe Amara," Jeremy suggested. Seeing her son glance over at Laina with so much love in his eyes soothed Ronica's heart.

"Right," Ronica agreed. "And if it's true, it will put everyone's mind to rest because I know Carina has been living with the worry that the biological mother could appear and make trouble."

"She might have." Laina made a face. "You know, later."

Ronica shivered at the idea. "I think if Joni had meant to come back into Amara's life, she would have left her with Natalie."

"Maybe she left her with the Sayers because of her spinal issues."

"Maybe. Those should have been seen on an ultrasound while she was expecting." Ronica liked thinking that Joni wanted the best for her daughter and at the same time wanted to spare her mother the hardship of caring for a physically disabled child, but Joni's treatment of Natalie had never shown that kind of care. More likely, she hadn't wanted anyone to force her to take further responsibility or have anyone judge her actions. But that wasn't something Ronica would say aloud.

"Thankfully, the effects so far are more minimal than the Sayers first expected," Ronica said instead. "She may still need surgery, but the Sayers are prepared for that."

They were silent for several minutes then, but as they stared up the road to their houses, Laina said to Ronica, "Hey, want to come eat dinner with us?"

"How about a rain check? I appreciate the invitation, but I really need to say hi to Moona Lisa, then take a long bath and crash in my own bed."

Laina laughed. "Okay. Rain check. Jeremy's grilling anyway, so I can't guarantee how good it will be." As Jeremy was excellent at grilling, they all laughed aloud.

"Don't worry about milking Moona Lisa," Jeremy added. "We'll do that and put the milk away."

He had taken the milk to the Butter Cake Café while she was away, but she'd need to make cheese soon with the extra and also butter from the cream. "Thanks, son. I'll take you up on that." Ronica knew she was fortunate to have them both.

Why then did her heart feel like a weight was sitting on it?

Out in the barn, Moona Lisa greeted her with moos. "I missed you too, girl." She scratched the place between her horns that the Holstein enjoyed most until her phone buzzed. It was Josiah, asking if she'd made it home safely, a follow-up from that afternoon when he'd asked if she had a ride back to town. Seeing his question somehow hurt more. He needed to stop with the personal questions, and she'd have to find a way to tell him she needed space.

I'm home safely, she texted. *Going to clean up and relax.* Hopefully, he'd take the hint and wouldn't text back anything she'd feel obligated to answer.

After a long bath that was a little too hot, Ronica dressed in a warm pair of clean sweats that she could also wear to bed. The past few days—no, the entire past week and a half had been emotionally taxing, and she was grateful to settle down on her own family room couch in front of the television.

She lay back, staring at the blank screen. It had been entirely too long since she'd had to decide on something to watch. For the past few years, it had always been something to entertain Fletcher. When he'd gone to sleep, she caught up on chores or occasionally listened to a mystery on audio book. But now the rest of her life stretched in front of her with time to fill. It was scary but also a little liberating. She hadn't been on her own since she was nineteen.

Her mind wandered to the wedding. She'd already put her idea for most of Laina's decorations in motion, and even ordered her own red dress from Joni's Dress Shop, though now she should probably make sure Natalie would still be able to deliver on time. That reminded her to touch base with Natalie again. They'd had a long chat on the phone that afternoon, but a little text to let her know she was thinking about her would remind her she was available any time she needed to talk.

After sending the text, she considered getting herself something to eat. There were plenty of leftovers in the fridge that might not have gone bad during her time away, and also a couple of full casseroles in the freezer. But she decided she didn't want any of it. She simply wanted to stare at the blank television and listen to the silence.

The ringing of the doorbell pulled her from a light doze. For a moment, she was tempted to stay put under the multi-colored afghan Fletcher's mother had made. It was soft and fuzzy after years of washing, and Ronica loved the regular pattern and thinking about her mother-in-law, who had crocheted every evening as she sat with her family in this very room.

The bell rang again, finally propelling Ronica to her feet. She suspected it was Laina, coming with food anyway. But instead of Laina standing on her porch, it was Josiah wearing a black coat, his dark face and short-cropped hair blending in with the night.

"Josiah! What a surprise." His text hadn't mentioned coming over.

"Can I come in?"

She looked behind him. Night had fallen and there was no sign of life except for the few lights on at Jeremy's. Laina would likely stay there for an hour or more, and if they saw Josiah's car, they wouldn't automatically assume the worst.

She stepped back. "Sure. I was thinking about getting something to eat. You hungry?"

He hesitated a moment as if considering. "Yes, I think so. I can't be long, though. I have to get back to Charlie."

She led him down the hallway to the kitchen. "So you talked to him? How did that go?"

"It went well. Thanks to you."

"That's good." She gestured to the table. "Have a seat and let me take a look at what I've got. I can always whip something else up, though, if it doesn't sound good." She was already going over the contents of her freezer in her mind. The casseroles would take too long, but she had some thinner steaks frozen flat that would be easy to thaw in the microwave and then fry.

"Wait." Something in his voice froze her into place.

She turned slowly to face him, fearing what she would see. To her surprise, he was grinning—a real grin like those he'd worn while playing chess with Fletcher.

"I have good news, and maybe I should have texted you, but I wanted to be with you to see your reaction. And I wanted it to be official."

"Good news?" With the way things had been going so far this year, it took a moment for her to process that.

His grin grew wider. He had the best smile, with full lips that invited kissing, though she'd never let herself dwell on that before and couldn't now because he wasn't free.

"Yes." He reached into his coat pocket and withdrew a paper folded into thirds like a letter.

She unfolded it—and recognized an addendum to his divorce papers.

"Olivia signed it when she got home on Saturday. And it was recorded right after I texted you before you left Panna Creek. I am no longer married."

This was so far from Ronica's expectation that she could do nothing but stare. "Olivia gave you the divorce? But . . . what about her cancer? What made her change her mind?"

"She says she doesn't want me to hate her and tarnish her memory when I talk about her with Charlie."

"You wouldn't do that."

He shrugged. "I would try not to, but it would be difficult. It might be that she's more worried about how not signing makes her look to Charlie when he knew our marriage failure was her fault and not mine. At any rate, she doesn't believe she's going to make it past this summer, so she's moving to Lincoln with a cousin of hers that she'll pay to take care of her. Or a second cousin, rather. I have to take Charlie there every weekend when she's doing well and for a week at a time between treatments during the summer, if it's workable for her and if he's amenable."

Ronica blinked. "That doesn't sound like Olivia."

"No, it doesn't. I think you impressed her."

"Me?" This was even more surprising.

"You are always impressive." He shrugged off his coat, letting it drop to the round table, and stepped closer.

All at once, she was keenly aware that they were alone—the first time alone when neither of them was married. She was also acutely aware of how she looked, standing there in her sweats with no makeup and her hair having dried uncombed, while he was in a well-cut suit that made him look every bit the mayor that he was.

"Ronica," he said, his voice a whisper now that spread through her, seeping into her pores and running through her veins, slowly at first, then ramping up speed until it reached her heart, pushing it into overdrive.

"Yes?" Her voice was breathy.

"May I kiss you? Please?" The need in his voice was enticing, calling her to fill it.

"Yes."

He reached out and pulled her into his arms, his eyes never leaving her face. "I've dreamed of this for too long. Or rather, tried not to dream of it."

"Me too."

His lips touched hers. Again she had the sensation of his essence seeping into her, filling her with light and love. At first, she felt awkward because it had been so long since she'd kissed a man. That made her think of Fletcher and how he'd known from the beginning that she'd move on. And here she was, doing just that.

She almost pulled away. But Josiah's tongue slid along her bottom lip, tasting and soothing her. She wrapped her arms around his neck, stretching up to meet him. His body seemed to form to hers perfectly, though he was significantly taller. The kiss deepened, and he explored her mouth before his lips wandered to her neck and the little place behind her ears that made delicious goose bumps form all over her body. She shuddered and drew his mouth back to hers, kissing him with more passion.

Too soon, he drew away, his dark eyes tumultuous. "That's really something."

She laughed. "Why? Because white girls don't know how to kiss?"

"No. Because I feel like I'm twenty years old again."

"You ain't seen nothing yet." She kissed him again, then captured his bottom lip between her teeth. With a little groan, he pulled her closer and kissed her long and deep until their breathing was erratic, and Ronica was having all kinds of ideas that would ordinarily cause her to blush. This time she was the one who pulled away.

Josiah's eyes roamed over her face as if drinking it in. "You are so beautiful."

It was the right thing to say, and at that moment she felt beautiful, even in sweats and with uncombed hair. Beautiful and flushed with her love. Maybe it was true that there was no greater beauty to a good and decent man than a woman who loved him.

Without warning, Josiah stepped back and went down on one knee.

"Josiah, what are you doing?" Panic blotted out some of her euphoria.

"Actually, something Olivia told me to do. Something I wish I could have done thirty-three years ago when you first came to town." He paused for five of her pounding heartbeats. "Ronica, I love you with all that I am, and I have loved you since we first met. Will you marry me?"

Joy spread through her in an unexpected wave. "Oh, Josiah . . . I love you too. So much." She hesitated. "But do you really think you should be asking this now? You've been divorced less than a day, and I've only been a widow for eleven. You know people will talk."

He arched one of his black brows, and she couldn't help reaching out to smooth it. "Since when do you care about what people say?"

He was right about that, but this seemed different somehow. "I don't want anyone to think ill of you. And with Olivia's cancer and Fletcher only just gone, people who don't know us, and even those who do . . . there will be a lot of talk." No one had lived their lives or understood what they'd been through with their spouses, so they would only see the timing.

"I don't care," he said. "Fifty-two is too old to worry about that, so I'm still asking. Ronica, will you marry me?"

"When? In three months? Four?" Her mind raced. How long would be appropriate given their situation and his role as mayor? Plus, she wouldn't want her engagement to overshadow Jeremy and Laina's day, or even Keisha and Xander's.

"That's way too long." His grin widened. "How about tonight? Or tomorrow, rather. We'll elope. I know a district judge in Panna Creek who will waive the three-day waiting period. We can grab him and his wife to be our witnesses. Then we'll keep it a secret until the time is right. In fact—" he raised his eyebrows suggestively "—sneaking around might be a lot of fun."

Laughter bubbled up inside her. "You're crazy. You know that, right?"

"I am finally free to let myself love you, that's all." Spoken in his resonant voice, it was the most romantic and sexy thing she'd ever heard.

"Well, tomorrow is Joni's funeral, and you're far too well-known in Panna Creek. People will find out." Was she actually considering this?

His face sobered. "Then we'll go to another town in Kansas where no one knows us. It can't be Lincoln because, unlike Kansas, Nebraska has a six-month waiting period after a divorce."

"You're really serious about this." Serious enough to look up legal requirements in at least two different states.

"I don't want to spend another day apart from you." He rose and kissed her again. "But I'm never letting you go, and I will wait for as long as you want."

Her head whirled as she responded to his kiss. What was she waiting for? Ronica already knew she wanted to be with this man for the rest of her life. She'd made a choice once before to give him up, and it had been the right thing to do. But now there was nothing holding her back, and if she didn't take a chance, who knew what awaited them around the corner? If she'd learned anything from Fletcher's dementia, Olivia's cancer, and Joni's death, it was that life could change in an instant. And like she'd told Jeremy, sometimes you needed to act with your heart.

"Okay," she said, pushing him back a little so she could think. "Give me until after Valentine's Day and the kids' wedding to figure things out. That's only three weeks away. Then you can ask me again."

He punched his fist in the air and whooped. "Ha! I knew I'd wear you down. Or is it because I'm just that great of a kisser?"

She laughed. "I'm not sure. Why don't we try some more and find out?"

CHAPTER 19

On Tuesday afternoon, Natalie sat on the bed in Joni's old room next to a box of mementos that Caleb had brought back from where she'd been staying with Nolan. Aside from the box, the room was the same as when Joni had left. Well, except it was clean. Clothes were still in the closet, her lesser worn ones, as well as shoes and costume jewelry. Sewing supplies and materials still filled the top shelf of the closet. Nothing of great value. Natalie would have to go through everything in the room one day and decide what to keep or give away. But not today.

On Tuesday afternoon, Natalie sat on the bed in Joni's old room next to a box of mementos that Caleb had brought back from where she'd been staying with Nolan. Aside from the box, the room was the same as when Joni had left. Well, except it was clean. Clothes were still in the closet, her lesser worn ones, as well as shoes and costume jewelry. Sewing supplies and materials still filled the top shelf of the closet. Nothing of great value. Natalie would have to go through everything in the room one day and decide what to keep or give away. But not today.

The small funeral earlier that morning had been healing because so many people—her friends—offered sympathy for her heartache. They recounted stories and memories of happier times, mostly when Joni was a child. When shared, her grief seemed lighter, and even though she knew Joni had chosen to walk away from her, Natalie also knew she'd been a good mother.

And that was enough.

She hadn't gone with Caleb yesterday when he went to collect the items. She didn't want to see the place where her daughter had chosen to spend the last months of her life, slowly dying instead of reaching out to her family for help. He'd also brought Nolan back with him so he could attend the funeral, and he was staying at the Butter Cake Café in one of the three bedrooms Maggie rented out on the second floor. Caleb had been in contact with his parents, and Nolan told her today that they'd bought him an airplane ticket to visit them that weekend. Natalie didn't know if he'd turn his life around or end up like Joni, but at least he had another chance.

"Mom."

She looked up to see Kenley standing in the doorway. She'd taken the week off work. Family grief leave, or something of that sort. "Yes?"

"Are you okay?"

"Yeah, I am." Natalie smiled. "Did I tell you thanks for being here this weekend? It really helped me." She wanted to beg her to stay longer, maybe even to move back to Forgotten or at least to Panna Creek, but she'd learned her lesson about expectations. Kenley had her life to live, and she didn't want to put too much pressure on her.

Kenley laughed as she came further into the room. "About a million times. You don't have to thank me. I'm glad to be here."

A knot formed in Natalie's stomach as she worried that even her thanking might push Kenley away. Would she always worry about others cutting her off? She took a deep breath. Maybe, but for now, she would deal with that concern privately, because most of all, she wanted Kenley to be happy.

"I was wondering about what we should do with the phone." Kenley waved it at her.

Natalie had forgotten about the phone. "Dad said it will likely sync with her computer and that a guy at the station will figure it out."

"Good, I'm betting there are a lot of photos inside."

"Probably."

"Any word on the DNA test?"

"It'll be weeks before we get the results." Natalie swung from the sweetest hope to the deepest despair when thinking about whether or not Amara was her granddaughter. Her mood seemed to change hourly and sometimes by the minute. She wanted it to be true.

Kenley sat on the bed and stared down into the box between them. "This is all Dad brought back?"

"Plus the laptop and her sewing machine."

Kenley chuckled. "She was never without her sewing machine. But I'm actually surprised the boyfriend didn't hide the laptop to pawn."

Natalie was too, but she only smiled and drew out a book. "Looks like a journal, but Joni was never one to do much writing or reading. I think I'm afraid to open it."

Kenley held out her hand. "Want me?"

Natalie placed it in her hands. It opened to the last entry, which had a calendar penned on it. Even from her position, Natalie could see that at least several days were marked BAD in large, red lettering. Kenley brought the book closer, turning back a few pages where more calendars filled the space. "It says drinking above it, so I think she was trying to quit. Look. Here are the days she succeeded, those marked with a heart, and the days marked BAD are the days she didn't follow through." There were far fewer hearts than words, and an entire week marked BAD in November. That was the last time she'd written.

Kenley turned to the beginning, where they found pages and pages of clothing designs Joni had created. Natalie reached out to touch a particularly beautiful dress. "She had so much talent."

"She did," Kenley agreed. "I can put these in your computer electronically so you can keep them and maybe even make the dresses up to sell, but I don't think you should keep her drinking calendars."

Natalie had to agree. Those would only make her feel bad.

"Wait, look!" Between a group of designs, Kenley found a drawing, one of a baby in a car seat, wrapped in a quilt with a slip of paper tucked by the child's leg.

Natalie stared. "Do you think that's . . . ?"

"It has to be."

"Where's my phone?" Natalie felt the bed for it, opening the screen and snapping a picture of the drawing. She texted it to Carina Sayer with the words: *Found this in Joni's things. Does it look familiar?*

The response came back within a minute. *Looks like the car seat Amara was in. I have a picture we took for the police.*

Was anything on the paper? Natalie asked.

A date two days before. We thought it was her birthday.

Natalie read the texts aloud to Kenley and then added, "It might not mean anything."

"It means a lot." An odd note had entered Kenley's voice.

Natalie looked over to see her staring at Joni's phone, the screen now unlocked. "The numbers are on the paper," Kenley explained. "They're tiny but there."

Natalie typed to Carina: *Amara's birthday was the passcode to Joni's phone. I'm going to look through her pictures now.*

There were a lot of pictures dating back over the past year, but the dates soon became further between, as if she'd transferred photos to her computer to free up room. There was a picture of Natalie and Joni in the sewing room, laughing and holding up a dress they'd made for the Harvest Festival. Joni had been so beautiful in the blue gingham that matched her eyes and made a nice contrast with her beautiful blond hair. The difference in her face was notable from the later pictures—she was soft and glowing instead of skeletal and ill. Natalie remembered that time, and it had probably been right around five years ago at the end of September. She'd had so much hope for Joni then.

Several months earlier, the baby pictures began. Dozens of them, with and without Joni. That her daughter had chosen to go through labor alone and had a baby during her second estrangement from her family was heartbreaking to Natalie. She and Caleb would have lovingly welcomed her home and supported her. She started to sob—deep wrenching sobs that seemed to have no end.

"If only I would have been more understanding," she said between gasps. "Then she would have trusted me."

Kenley hugged her. "Oh, Mom, even if you had the biggest fight, she could have stopped it at any time. Don't I just tell you if you hurt my feelings? You always see it and understand when I explain. That's what families do. Joni just . . . she didn't want to ever be seen as wrong."

"I failed her."

"No," Kenley's voice was firm. "She failed you. Because whenever she needed something, you always came running."

"But why leave Amara at Doc's clinic? Why not let her family raise her?"

"Maybe Joni didn't want you to know how much she messed up. And there are physical issues. You and Dad are close to retirement. Do you really want to be raising a child with medical needs?"

"I want a grandchild." Natalie could have bitten her tongue after saying the words because she didn't want Kenley to think she was talking pointedly at her. Everything she said these days felt wrong because of the estrangement. She didn't know if anything she felt was even valid.

But Kenley laughed. "Of course you do. And Amara can still be that, right?"

Natalie sniffed. "Doc's only about ten years younger than we are."

"Yeah, but Carina is younger than him." Kenley took her hands. "Mom, this is a blessing. We have a second chance to love a part of Joni. You can teach her to sew and make her prom dresses. Carina and Doc are good people. They'll let you be in her life." She paused a moment before adding, "But in case you're thinking about it, there is no judge in Kansas who would reverse their adoption."

"Oh, I would never . . ." Yet hadn't that crossed her mind? Of course it would be wrong to take Amara from the only family she'd ever known. Natalie would never put her through that. "What if Carina doesn't want us involved?"

Kenley laughed. "Carina? She's your friend. I say give her a chance. She has that whole Hispanic vibe going on, you know? The more family, the better."

Natalie smiled through her tears. "Maybe you're right."

The faint ringing of the doorbell sounded in the house, and Natalie instinctively wiped the tears from her face, though she knew Caleb would get the door. It was likely a casserole from a neighbor or church member, and they would understand if she didn't come to greet them.

She let out a sigh. "Okay. I feel so shaky, and I don't know why."

"You've been through a lot." Kenley frowned. "Mom, I'm sorry I haven't been around more. I've been so busy."

Natalie reached out to gently touch her face. "Oh, sweetie, I'm the one who's sorry. It's a hard adjustment going from raising you guys to letting you live your own lives, and I know I need to focus on making my life full even when you're busy. You're not supposed to take care of me like that."

Kenley hugged her again. "I will always need you."

It was on the tip of Natalie's tongue to ask Kenley to swear she'd never cut her off, but that implied mistrust. It implied she expected Kenley to change into a person she wasn't. Saying such a thing wasn't fair or kind. "I will always need you too."

Caleb appeared in the doorway to the room, looking hesitant. Natalie smiled and said, "We got into the phone. We found photos of Amara."

He didn't speak but moved forward, and it was only then that she saw he wasn't alone. Carina and Doc were with them. And Amara too. Natalie stared at them in shock.

"We thought we'd come over," Carina said, "and introduce Amara to her new grandparents."

"There's no need to wait for the DNA test now," Doc added.

"Oh." The faint word escaped Natalie's mouth like a sigh. Her gaze went eagerly to Amara. She was slender and beautiful, with her blue eyes so very large in her oval face. Before she'd started kindergarten, she played in this very room whenever Natalie hosted the Ladies Auxiliary meetings. Natalie had even babysat her on occasion. How could she have missed Joni's face staring back at her all these years?

"Hi, Amara," she greeted the child softly.

"Hi." Her gaze darted to the doll shelf near the window. "Can I play with the dolls?"

"Of course." Natalie wanted to tell her she could have them all, but maybe it was better not to overwhelm her all at once.

"Honey, do you remember what we told you at home?" Carina said.

Amara stopped halfway to the window. "I have new grandparents?"

"Yes. Chief McColl and Mrs. McColl. But you can call them Grandma and Grandpa."

Natalie blinked back tears so she wouldn't scare Amara. This was more than she could have asked for.

Amara's little face puckered. "Like my other grandma and grandpa?"

Carina glanced at her husband and then at Natalie. "She calls Davy's parents Grandma and Grandpa and my parents Abuela and Abuelo."

"She could use Granny and Gramps," Kenley quipped, her eyes glinting in amusement.

"Uh . . ." Carina said doubtfully, missing the sarcasm.

"How about calling me Grandma Nat?" Natalie said. "Or at least we can begin there. And you can call him . . ." Natalie looked at Caleb.

"I kind of like Gramps," he said. Everyone laughed.

Amara smiled shyly. "Okay. I might forget, though." She glanced longingly at the dolls, and Natalie knew that hugs and kisses and that sort of thing would have to wait until they spent a lot more time together.

"Go ahead," Natalie encouraged. Then she couldn't help adding, "You can even take them home."

Amara's eyes widened. "Really?"

"Just one," Carina said. "Grandma Nat will need to keep some here for you to play with when you come to visit."

Natalie looked at her gratefully. "Oh, right. I guess I wasn't thinking." But now that Carina had mentioned it, she was already envisioning buying a million toys and fixing up the room for a little girl to maybe sleep over every now and then when her parents needed a night out.

They were all quiet for a moment as Amara played with the dolls. After a while, Kenley went to kneel beside her. "This one was actually mine when I was little," she said. "I'm Aunt Kenley, by the way."

Dragging her eyes from Kenley and Amara, Natalie rose and took Carina's hands. "Thank you."

"No, thank you." Carina's wide dark eyes held her gaze. "Amara is the light of our lives and if not for you two and Joni, we wouldn't have her. We are happy to share our little girl. There is no such thing as too much love for a child."

They both wiped away tears but discreetly so as not to alarm Amara. And when the Sayers left an hour later, Amara was clutching a new doll that had been her mother's, though no one had yet spoken about Joni—that would come later. Natalie felt happier than she had in a very long time. She would always mourn her child, but Amara was a blessing, and she would not let the past steal their future.

Deciding she might finally be ready to break the unintentional fast she'd been on today, she headed to the kitchen, but her ringing phone distracted her. It was Ronica.

"Hello?"

"How are you?" Ronica asked. "And be honest. Can I come get you? We can drive around or go out to dinner."

"No, I'm fine. Guess what happened?" The story came out in a rush, and Natalie found herself grateful all over again for the unexpected blessing of Amara.

"I'm so happy for you!" Ronica nearly crowed. "This is fantastic news. You are going to be the best grandma ever!"

"Thank you." Natalie felt her grin might actually break her face with its wideness.

"Well, I should probably hang up right now," Ronica said. "But I know you'll never forgive me if I don't tell you my own news."

"Of course I'll forgive you." Natalie could forgive anything now that she'd been given a second chance.

"Olivia signed the divorce papers, and they went through yesterday. I was going to mention it at the funeral, but it seemed rather . . . you know, self-centered after all you've been through."

"Well, paint me green and call me a pickle." Natalie sank into a kitchen chair, shaking her head. "That doesn't sound like Olivia."

"She apparently has her reasons, and one of them is that she doesn't want Josiah to remember her poorly to Charlie, or I guess for Charlie to remember her poorly for roping Josiah into taking care of her and not going through with the divorce."

"That makes sense, I guess."

"And I think she hated us seeing her like that. She'll be staying in Lincoln and paying a distant cousin to watch her." Ronica hesitated. "But there's something else. Something important. You've got so much going on right now that it's selfish of me to even bring it up, but I know both of us will regret it later if I don't tell you."

"Spill away!" Natalie ordered. It felt good to be interested in something besides her own drama.

"It's the utmost secret. Like you can't even tell Caleb because we all know he can't keep a secret unless it's related to policework."

"Right. Not telling him. I'm all yours."

But what Ronica told her made Natalie pull the phone away from her ear and stare at it in utter shock.

CHAPTER 20

Ronica looked around the reception room at City Hall with satisfaction. The place looked as she might have imagined it back in the day when it had been a ballroom. Couples danced in the open space or ate at tables along the edges. Everything was perfect, draped abundantly in pinks and reds. Even Ronica's mother-of-the-groom dress was red and made her look fantastic, Natalie having outdone herself with her sewing. Ronica and Pamela had worried that Laina would not stand out among all the red, even in her fantastic dress, but she did so amazingly, as all the guests had also been asked to wear red or pink, or black for the men. In stunning contrast, Laina looked like a fairy princess, and Jeremy in his white tuxedo was her prince.

Ronica's Kansas dirt cake was a huge hit, taking up six small round tables to display. She and Maggie had made the individual cakes ahead of time, freezing them, and they had spent the hour before the wedding setting them up on electrically chilled metal plates, made by Maggie's husband and covered with red tablecloths. Most of the important landmarks of Forgotten were represented, though with lots of reds and pinks added to tie in with the décor.

Josiah came up and extended a hand. "May I have this dance?"

Ronica couldn't stop herself from looking around covertly as she stood. "Okay. But I thought we were going to keep a low profile."

His smile widened. "It's a wedding, and we're friends. Besides, I'm divorced now. No reason not to dance with a pretty widow."

"You're enjoying this."

He chuckled. "Just wait until you see what I might do if I get you alone in the coat room. You are ravishing in that red dress."

She blurted out a laugh. For the past three weeks, they'd been secretly dating, and she felt as if she hadn't stopped smiling. Eventually, someone was going to notice the sparks between them. But so far it was delicious and fun.

Something bumped into her, and Ronica turned to find Amara Sayer giggling in a beautiful pink princess dress. Instead of her normal blue alicorn, she was carrying the pink one Nolan had brought to the hospital.

"Sorry," she said with a giggle. "I'm trying to play hide-and-seek."

Natalie appeared behind her. "There you are, cutie."

"You really are cute," Ronica told the child. "And that dress is amazing."

Amara spun around for her. "Grammy made it. She's going to teach me how."

"Grammy?" asked Ronica with a laugh.

"That's what she's chosen." Natalie shrugged. "It's perfect." And they were off again through the dancers.

The music slowed, as if just for them, and Josiah stepped closer, cradling her with familiarity.

"I was surprised to see Olivia here," she said as he swirled her around.

"You and me both. Apparently, she wants to make sure Keisha's wedding next month outdoes this one."

"Rather difficult since this is the largest venue around."

"Oh, but she's rented out all of Gandolf's. And they are taking the opportunity to do a bit of renovating."

"Wow, really?" Gandolf's Ravioli Restaurant was one of the nicer old buildings on Forgotten's Main Street, and if updated and decorated correctly, the wedding would probably be the event of the year, but the only reason Olivia would fill the space was because everyone loved Keisha, Xander, and Josiah. Well, that and excellent free food, which it would be unless Olivia attempted to serve the questionable ravioli. "That's very interesting."

"I thought so too. I hear the owners want the money to attract a better chef so they can finally sell good ravioli, but I bet they're already sorry they signed the contract." He didn't sound too worried, and neither was she.

"They'll know to go to Keisha if there's a problem. She's got her head on straight."

"Well, for what it's worth, I think Olivia has mellowed." Josiah leaned down and whispered in her ear, "She asked me yesterday when I was going to propose to you."

It was all she could do not to lean into his warmth and kiss him. "And you said?"

"I told her—politely, of course—that it was none of her business."

"Good answer." But that didn't answer the question Ronica really wanted to ask. She'd told him to wait until the wedding was over to ask her again, and now that she had watched Jeremy and Laina exchange vows, all she could think about was Josiah and how seeing and kissing him every day made her want more.

They were now dancing close to the edge of the reception hall that was farthest away from the door. The music stopped, and he reached for her hand. The next moment, he was pulling her into a closet—no, it was a hidden door.

"What?" she asked with a little laugh.

He grinned. "I wasn't kidding about the coat closet, only this one was actually the fainting room back in the late eighteen hundreds." He reached over and locked the door. "The molding on the door makes it blend into the wall."

"A fainting closet?" She stared at him doubtfully.

"Apparently, it was a big thing then."

"How'd you even know that it was here?"

"I'm the mayor," he said with a straight face. "I know everything about this place." He cracked another smile. "Or at least the city engineer does."

She laughed, but her amusement faded as she noted the dim lighting, flowers on the antique tables around the room, and flower petals on the floor. On an end table next to an antique sofa was a bottle of something chilling on ice.

"You've been busy," she said.

"I've been impatient," he corrected.

"I wouldn't say that."

This time when he knelt, he drew out a box with a ring inside. "Ronica, will you marry me this Friday in Marysville?"

She examined the ring, a thick eternity band full of channel-cut, rectangular diamonds. Beautiful, but not the traditional wedding ring. Of course, she had barely taken her old one off tonight for the first time.

"It's an anniversary band," he said. "Something I think you can wear right away without questions."

"I love it."

"And me?"

"I love you too." She leaned over to kiss him. "I will marry you, Josiah."

He slipped the ring onto her finger, then stood, pulling her to his chest. "Just to be sure. You heard I asked for this Friday, right?"

"Yes."

On the Friday after Valentine's Day, Ronica and Josiah were married in a tiny church in Marysville, Kansas. But they weren't alone. Natalie McColl was there, as well as Laina's mother, Pamela Cox, to be witnesses.

Josiah had laughed at her need to include them. "You know, it may not remain a secret if someone besides us knows."

But she was adamant that they wouldn't tell anyone, and besides, they'd both known since his first proposal. It was going to be hard hiding their marriage from Jeremy and Laina, but she was sure they'd be wrapped up in each other enough not to notice her going off for the weekend more often, and so far they hadn't been concerned with Josiah's car occasionally being parked outside her house during the day.

Ronica wore a simple off-white, calf-length dress from Natalie's store, fitted by Natalie herself, who had insisted on gifting it to her. Pamela had brought a fresh bouquet of lilies for Ronica to hold, and Josiah was as handsome and distinguished as always in a black suit.

The ceremony was simple and didn't require long paragraphs of undying love, which to Ronica didn't seem right with Fletcher being gone such a short time. Maybe when they held the official wedding later in the year, she'd feel differently, but she was old enough to know that those things wouldn't make or break the relationship. It was the daily in and out that would determine their success.

When Josiah kissed her after the pastor announced them as husband and wife, she knew this was the right thing to do. No one knew what tomorrow held, and she was going to embrace his love for as long as they had together.

Natalie grinned at her as they headed into a restaurant for a celebratory dinner. "You could have had the wedding at the Butter Cake Café, you know. Your friends wouldn't have judged you."

Ronica leaned toward Natalie, giving her a side hug. "I have loved Josiah for a long time now, but I'm not ready to announce that to the world just yet."

She nodded. "I understand. Fletcher was a good man."

"He was."

Someday soon—maybe in a couple of months—she and Josiah would start dropping hints about dating. Then they'd get officially engaged. For now, though, he was all hers, and she wanted to keep it that way.

They spent their wedding night at a Marysville hotel, where they would stay the entire weekend, since Charlie was with his mother in Lincoln.

"I love you so much," he whispered when they were finally alone. "And I'm never letting go. Remember that. No matter what."

"Good," she said. "I like that just fine."

Josiah's arms went around her, kissing her until her pulse raced. Together they began exploring each other's bodies, learning all the nooks and crannies. He was hers. All hers. And she was his.

This was only the beginning.

HISTORY OF FORGOTTEN
and James and Chelsea Morgan

In the late 1850s in Missouri, James Morgan, the son of a wealthy farmer, and Chelsea Fortson, the daughter of an important abolitionist cattle rancher, fell in love and wanted to marry, but their fathers were sworn enemies, divided on the issue of slavery, so they separated their children, forbidding them to associate or fall in love—as if such a thing could be mandated.

Not that their fathers didn't try. James was made to travel to Virginia, where his father, who had been elected to government office, moved in an attempt to influence the politicians there in favor of slavery. Chelsea was sent to what would eventually become Kansas to live with relatives, who, like Chelsea's father, were firmly on the side of Kansas entering the Union as a free state. For three years, James and Chelsea lived apart with nothing more than secret letters passed between them, aided by loyal friends and servants.

James worked hard managing one of his father's farms, and he eventually put together enough funds to get himself to Kansas to ask Chelsea to run away with him. He showed up on her doorstep, his identity disguised, and she packed a bag and left with him that same night. When their marriage was discovered, both of them were disowned by their disgruntled families.

They thought that would be the end of their struggle, and their families would eventually come to accept their union. Unfortunately, they married in early 1861, near the same time Kansas was formed and became a free state. Embittered by his defeat, James's father considered his son's marriage an affront to his entire way of life, and it wasn't enough to simply disinherit James for his betrayal. Instead, he sent a posse after him, made up of the wildest, ferocious, and murderous men. They found James in Kansas and shot him. Chelsea, eight months pregnant with her first child, threw herself in front of him. Her beauty was such that these ruffians took pity on her and left him to bleed out in her arms.

Chelsea, accustomed to tending wounded cattle, stopped the bleeding and called for a doctor. James's leg had to be amputated, and he nearly died of infection, but Chelsea slowly nursed him back to health, all the while keeping his survival a secret. She wrote to her father, begging for his help and forgiveness and telling him about his grandchild. Only years later did she learn that he'd died after being shot by his pro-slavery enemies. Her brother inherited their large ranch and, being a greedy man, tore up her letter so he wouldn't have to share.

When no help came, Chelsea earned a living making ravioli at a restaurant during the day and sewing dresses late into the night until James was finally well enough to come out of hiding. By then, they wanted nothing to do with their families, so they took off to the northern part of Kansas near the border of what would become Nebraska. They built a one-room cabin and began to farm. Thirteen children were born to them, and Chelsea often walked the fields at night with her children, hand-in-hand, teaching them the harvest songs.

When people passing through the area asked James and Chelsea where they were from, they claimed they'd been gone so long that they'd forgotten because they feared word might get back to their families. Most of the couple's thirteen children married people from nearby towns and returned to help farm the land. The town became known as Forgotten, a place of a new life for all those who had been or wanted to be forgotten, and where thirteen was the luckiest number.

To this day, weddings, birthdays, and other special events are always planned for the thirteenth. Every year in Forgotten, the town celebrates the first harvest by singing the harvest songs and reenacting the story of James and Chelsea Morgan with the hope that Chelsea will bless the harvest for another year.

Legend has it that people who stay in Forgotten, especially those running from their past or those who want to forget, usually end up finding themselves.

Rachel Branton has worked in publishing for over thirty years. She loves writing women's fiction and traveling, and she hopes to write and travel a lot more. As a mother of six great kids and with a growing number of grandchildren, it's not easy to find time to write, but the semi-ordered chaos of her life gives her a constant source of writing material. She's been known to wear pajamas all day when working on a deadline, and is often distracted enough to burn dinner—well, when she remembers to cook it. She lives in central Florida and loves going to the beach with her husband, hanging out with her grandchildren, and riding very tall rollercoasters.

Under the name Rachel Branton, she writes romance, romantic suspense, and women's fiction. Rachel also writes urban fantasy, paranormal romance, and science fiction under the name Teyla Branton. For more information or to sign up to hear about new releases, please visit www.RachelBranton.com.